HOME

the story of her girl

Laura Ross

Staten House

Staten House

Printed in the United States of America

First Printing, 2022

Photo credit: Anna Shvets

ISBN 979-8-89778-058-7

Staten House
447 Broadway

2nd Floor

New York, NY 10013

www.statenhouse.com

To my Readers,
You keep me writing.
Thank you.

CONTENTS

It's okay, lady
Everything's alright
I'll protect us
With all my might
Erase the fright
Put it under the bed
Throw it in trash cans
So, I can't even find it
All that fright
That materialized in head
Will haunt the dreams
And scare you instead
So, leave milady alone, monster
Or you'll answer to me
I won't just throw you away
Because, to me, you're not so
Frightening

Prologue

"I don't think you understand what you are to me."

Kimberly's small smile grew coy as she stared into my eyes. Our lips met in a kiss, so brief, so flickering, it almost felt as if it didn't happen at all. A harsh wind blew by us as Monday's moon shone brightly above our heads, the impact of the gust flushed our bodies close together, her front meeting mine.

"Ooh, s-sorry." She muttered, embarrassed by her actions.

Since we were eye level, it was no problem for me to caress her cheek with my palm. My sweet Kimmy, I thought lovingly. God she was all I wanted. All I needed. And the only place I ever wanted to be.

I couldn't hide the smile that tugged at my lips.

"Babydoll, don't apologize. I knew you just couldn't help yourself from being as close to me as possible. I know it completes you."

Despite the wintry Virginia winds, a flash of heat surged to her pale cheeks as she slapped me playfully on my shoulder. "You *complete* me with your closeness? Now you're just fishing." She laughed.

I chewed on my lip as I watched her head tilt back with laughter. Gosh, I don't know what was with me tonight, but her every move seemed graceful, her every word I clung to.

I chuckled and tightened my arms around her slim frame. "Fishing? But aren't I just sooo cute?"

She smirked. "You're incorrigible."

I smiled devilishly. "And you're my everything."

Her face turned stone serious as she assessed mine. Her arms tightened round my neck as she lowered her lips close to mine. "Don't do this to me."

I frowned slightly, and realized the events of the day and how much I needed her to see I now meant it.

My thick curls blew in the wind as another gust of wind blew straight through my thicker arms, and I allowed all the humor to drain from my next words.

Savoring the delight within her arms, I leaned in close to press my lips to her ear.

"Wherever you're not, my soul is lost." I said, praying my words could stretch the distance I feared grew between us.

She looked away, and I thought I caught a tear forming in her eyes. My hand shot out to gently grasp her chin, bringing her eyes to meet mine. No way was she running from this.

"You *are* everything." I whispered, falling and feeling myself become captive in her eyes and enraptured by her love. "You are HOME..."

I

GHOSTS

I didn't like living in the past. Truly, I didn't, but with this cracked brain of mine all bets were off when it came to time, space, and reality.

"Vonnie, want to walk Mommy somewhere?" Helen, my mother, asked as we strode down the littered streets of DC.

She, my twin brother Michael, and I were walking home from school and it was a cloudy foreboding day. Almost as foreboding as the dark circles that lined Mommy's sunken eyes.

I stared up at her, confused. "Where?"

She made a point to avoid my eyes. "To a friend's house. For a favor."

At the mention of that haunting word, my blood chilled. I knew what this meant and I dreaded whatever this favor entailed this time.

"What friend?" Mikey cut in, his usual exuberant chattiness bursting to the surface as it always did. "And can I come, too?"

When no answer came from her, Mikey persisted, much against the warning look I shot him.

"Mommy? Did you hear me? I want to come with you guys!" He chirped; a small frown marred his chubby face.

Without warning, Mommy stopped. I paused a little ways behind them, but Mikey seemed not to notice Mommy's lack of footsteps behind him.

"Michael." She bit out.

He froze, the catchy nursery rhyme we learned in school that day silencing in his throat. "Yes, mommy?"

"What did I tell you about interfering?" Her tone was gentle, yet laden with menacing promise.

Mikey faced her, his eyes tinged with fear and a brazenness I wished I'd inherited. "You said not ever interfere with favors."

"And what else?" She goaded, slinking closer to him.

"Um," he hesitated, thinking. "Never ask questions. Ever."

Mommy's smile was like slow pouring acid as it twisted her face and promised danger. She knelt down before him and spoke to him softly, cupping his face. "Good boy. You remember the way home?"

"Home?!" He screeched, distraught as his eyes bounced between her and me. "No! I-I wanna go with Vonnie."

Instinctively, I squeezed my eyes shut. I knew what would happen whenever Mommy's limits were pushed. Tested. Especially by one of us.

I didn't see it, but heard the contact of flesh against flesh, intuiting the slap she delivered like clockwork.

"Mommy!" Mikey screamed again in frustration.

I opened my eyes again to bear witness to Mommy smack him again, regardless of the unwanted attention her actions garnered in broad daylight.

"No. Fucking. Questions." She growled, shaking his meek shoulders. "Look at me. Tell me you understand."

Mikey shook his head, his eyes trained only on me. There was a fierce resolve behind my little brother's stare, one I'd only seen when he was talking about dinosaurs.

"No!" He seethed, real close to her face. "Take me. Take me instead. Leave Vonnie alone!"

Another smack, before she snarled. "Mikey, you got one more time to—"

"Mikey!" I blubbered, hating how all this went so wrong so fast. My entire body trembled in fear and my little voice was no more than a squeak from underuse. I didn't speak. Everybody knew, Mikey was the voice between the two of us, and I kept quiet as much as *possible. I knew what kind of trouble talking could get you into. I knew it all too well.*

"Please..." I whispered brokenly. "I can do it. I'm okay!"

"Vonnie!" He shouted, fighting in Mommy's ironclad hold. "Get off of me, Mom!"

"Just...I'll..." I stuttered, unknowing the best words for the situation. My tongue often got tied like this.

Hating my uselessness, I turned and ran. Ran so far, and so long that my lungs protested against the sudden exertion.

"Vonnie!" Mommy called, and I could hear her running after me.

If I kept running, then the trouble wouldn't come. I wouldn't be the cause of hurting Mikey anymore. So, I kept running despite the frantic screams from my twin and mom that evening.

2

FREEDOM IN FRAGMENTS

"Vonnie, come back!" I heard my brother demand as I regained consciousness. My heart pounded furiously in my chest as realization of my actions dawned on me. If the spittle drooling down my face wasn't proof enough of my reprehensible behavior, then the heated glare from the red-headed guy three pews ahead of me was. *Oh no*, I cowered inwardly, I lost time again. I witnessed the preacher at the center of the dark room finish his closing remarks with a question.

"Would anyone near and dear to the departed like to share a few words?" The ancient old man asked in a dry voice that relayed just how used to this routine he'd likely become. The routine of delivering death speeches.

After a brief silence, a thin white woman stood up and walked over to center stage. Her flaming red hair were amongst her most notable features along with the black pantsuit that made her look celebrity gorgeous. Sad green eyes scanned the mournful crowd as she braced herself with the mic in her hands.

"Hello, everyone. I want to thank each of you for attending my mother's Going Home Ceremony." I'm immediately reminded of the many euphemisms southerners used in place of more deleterious specifics. Though it had only been five years since moving from DC to the small farm country on the outskirts of Richmond, there was still much left to be understood.

"While my family and I are excited to be back in my hometown," the redhead woman stated in a watery tone. "We're saddened to see such a pillar in our family depart this world. My mother and I..." her breath caught. "We didn't always see eye-to-eye, but I love her. I miss her. It wasn't supposed to be like this..."

She breaks down in her tears, her shoulders racking with previously restrained sobs and a torture I couldn't relate to. A younger girl, around my age or so, rushes by her side to comfort her while escorting her back to her seat.

Unlike the evident affection this woman, Aunt Stevie's daughter, had for her recently deceased mother, I didn't cry at my mother's funeral. The piece of stone in my chest didn't wither or soften an inch when I received her ashes in the mail from the women's prison in which she met her demise. That impenetrable block of stone didn't allow me to mention her name for fear of her ghost returning to me. That woman was Lucifer, Lucy the Evil for short, the unspeakable evil that had a hand in hardening my heart.

"She's still our mom, Vonnie." My brother's voice whispered from one of the rooms of the mega mansion that was my mind. *"We still love her, right?"*

"Leave me alone, Mikey." I snarl inwardly at my twin ghost who manifested sometime after my thirteenth birthday. *Our* thirteenth birthday.

Just my luck, and just like when he was alive, he pays me no mind as he continues scolding me from the mega mansion. *"Sorry, Vonnie. But it's true. She is still our mom, regardless of what she put us through. We can't keep trying to forget. She's a part of you. Of us."*

I take a deep steadying breath, hating to have this argument here of all places. *"You know this isn't fair, right? To bring HER up right now, during a time like this? We're at Aunt Stevie's funeral for heaven's sake!"*

A beat of silence passes before he whispers in my mind, *"I heard you. I know you were thinking about Mom's funeral, or lack thereof. It's okay."*

His tone is reassuring as my mind floats back to the memory of receiving the ashes in the mail. Devin, our eldest and half-brother, encouraged us to have a mini ceremony for Lucy the Evil shortly before we made the mandatory move to live with Mamma Dean in Richmond. A final moment to say goodbye, is what he called it. I sent him on a tampon run and made haste with that short time frame to flush her ashes down the toilet. Boy, was he furious with me, but I didn't care. I couldn't care. Not when that evil woman barely gave a care for any of her children. Why should we honor her when she did her best to destroy us?

"Fuck her." I growled, hating the tear that slipped down my cheek at the memory.

"It's okay," Mikey repeated softly. *"You're triggered right now. That's what this is, right?"*

"What are you even doing here?" I scoff, trying in earnest to ignore the dangerous road this conversation was taking. *"You shouldn't be here. You know I lose time if you stay too long..."*

He sighs. *"Right, sorry sis. It just felt like you needed me. Just...try to stay calm today, okay? This is supposed to be your day, too, remember?"*

Before I can respond, a tight squeeze of my hand reminds me of the here-and-now, of the weeping adoptive grandmother sitting beside me I regrettably zoned out to.

Hattie "Mamma Dean" Carlson leans over and whispers in my ear. "You all right, child? Stay awake, now."

"Yes," I chirp guiltily as I work to adjust my weary gaze on her. It appeared I lost time again while arguing with my stubborn twin brother. The crowd was dispersing now, which let me know that I was not fully present again to hear the latter half of the funeral.

I eye Mamma Dean apologetically, taking notice of her entire getup. She's outfitted in her Sunday's best: a long black dress and white shawl coupled with her DSW loafers make the plus sized woman look regal. Though in her eighties, she has an air about her that demands attention of the best kind. Not today, however, as her black attire is easily washed out amidst the sea of black clothes donned by the rest of the funeral party.

Her teary eyes examined me with suspicious concern.

"Okay...well, we're about to head back to the house for supper. You wouldn't mind showing our guests around the farm, would you?"

I frown at the mention of the new arrivals I vaguely remember her telling me about yesterday. Apparently, they're New Jersey transplants and distant relatives of Aunt Stevie's, Mamma Dean's nearest and dearest friend, but aside from the little information I recall of their origin city, there isn't much I remember about them. Were they even at the funeral?

I make haste to scan the large church hall. People are conversing and slowly exiting the now-over funeral ceremony. Who are these people? And if they did attend Aunt Stevie's funeral, where were they?

I open my mouth to voice these questions aloud to Mamma Dean, only to find her amidst a crowd of elderfolk, talking in hushed tones as they probably regaled tales of Aunt Stevie's memory. I notice Cousin Dan as one of the individuals Mamma Dean speaks with, and his rugged features and nearly leather skin that's been dried from too much sun crinkles under his sorrowful frown. He's Aunt Stevie's brother, a brooding White man of very little words who lived for two reasons and two reasons alone: to take care of his older sister Stevie and work the farm. My heart shrivels a little as I consider the hit to his life purpose, fear being the main obstacle keeping me from viewing the woman's body a couple of feet from me in her casket.

"Vivian, Jeremy, and Kimberly." Michael's voice hums dutifully in my head.

I jump from the suddenness of his intrusion. "What?"

He chuckles in that way of his before reiterating, *"Remember? Mamma Dean came to our room last week when we were playing video games to tell us that Aunt Stevie's daughter Vivian will be moving here to take care of her full time? Said she was bringing her two kids, Kimberly and Jeremy."*

Faint flashes of my adoptive granny come floating to the surface as I search the rooms in my Mind Mansion for recollection of her words.

"Vonnie," She calls from my bedroom door. "The chicken is almost ready. Oh, and don't forget Stevie's daughter will be coming to town soon. They apparently lost their house and need a place to stay. So, they're coming to live here and "take care" of Stevie full time." She overemphasizes the words in a spitefully mocking tone. "They don't know we taking care of each other just fine. Even though she got the dementia real bad now, she is still a capable adult!"

"Don't worry, Mamma Dean." I hear my voice from one of the Mind Mansion's rooms answer her with a smile. "I'll make sure they feel right at home when they get here. Leave it to me!"

Fury washes through me as just what really happened that day assails me.

"*Mikey...*" I warn the boy inwardly. "*What did I tell you about taking over? Don't ever do that—*"

"*Unless it's an emergency. I know, I know.*" He responds as if bored with the repeated warning. "*But Vonnie. Mamma Dean was so sad when she came to us that day. You were so involved with the video game and thoughts of Devin; I just decided it was the best for me to take over. To take the strain off you. That's all, I promise.*"

I slink back into the chair, breathing an aggrieved sigh at the mention of our estranged brother. Well, he wasn't really estranged as much as he was just missing from our lives. No, my life, I reminded myself. Shortly after we moved from DC and Devin's graduation, he decided to enlist in the Army without telling me about it. It was like one day he was here, living happily for once with us on the farm, and then he was gone. The brother I regarded as a second dad just up and vanished from the home we recreated out of nothing, in a flash. He said he didn't tell me until the day before his deployment date because he knew it would upset me. Well, he pegged that right, because it took a crowd of friends and family to pry me off him before he was to board the plane to South Carolina for basic training. That shattered me. Shattered my brain into the fragmented pieces of Mind Mansion Mikey manifested from. That day, I thought somberly, was the anniversary of his departure. It's been four years since I'd seen my big brother and my heart still aches from his absence. I remember feeling...really low when Mamma Dean came by that day. So low that I slunk into one of those spacious rooms in the Mind Mansion, so deep it felt like I'd been laying in cotton. Playing video games was how I coped with shit. How I got by with the ghosts that haunted me in my parent's and brothers' absences, as it felt like I was less alone when I immersed myself in RPG mode during a war game. Or pretended to be someone else in a simulation game. Gaming numbed the ache and prevented the stone in my chest from crumbling completely. During those times I couldn't pull myself out of one of those Mind Mansion rooms, I considered it an emergency. During which, I allowed my exuberant

brother to take over like he always loved. I gave
him full autonomy to get us through or out of
emotionally charged situations, and this seemed
to be an accord that worked for us.

Well, until now.

"*It wasn't an emergency, Mikey.*" I warned him. "*I
was...I was just a little tired. And sad. You know that
day was the anniversary of Devin's...*"

"*I know.*" He answers quickly, to my delight,
since I had no emotional strength to finish that
sentence. "*Sorry, Von.*"

"Are you normally this rude or is this funeral
just boring you extra?" A deep voice interrupts
the speech I was moments away from giving my
little brother, causing me to flinch and look in its
direction.

3

A MILLION MILES TO GO

"Huh?" I ask, more than a little perturbed by the derision in this stranger's voice.

The guy, the same one I recognized with flaming red hair glowering at me an hour ago from the far pews, is standing in front of me. His arms are folded and he's sporting a black suit and dangerously green eyes that glitter their disapproval. Of me.

He scoffs. "Hello? Earth to Rude Girl? You straight up fell asleep during my mom's eulogy. If my family's pain bores you that much, you were free to leave!"

I rear back, feeling the challenge as I stand to my feet to confront the ginger asshole. "First of all, nice to meet you. I'm Yvonne."

A confused frown twists his thin face as he regards my extended hand.

Even though he's looking at my hand as if it were a thing dragged from the swampy depths of a DC sewer, I don't move it. I don't dare back down from this entitled asshole.

After another moment of heated eye battling, he shakes it, and I resume my rant.

"Jeremy." He grumbles.

"Nice to meet you." I say again, drumming up all the syrupy sweetness I learned to lace with my words from my southern grandma. "Now, would you like I call you 'asshole,' 'entitled jerk,' or 'invading bastard who needs to mind his own business?' Since 'Jeremy' seems to be too decent a title for the guy who barged over here and called me out of my name."

Oh, if I had a camera I'd revel in the shock on his face and frame the picture on my bedroom wall. A token to treasure this moment where I taught this irate son of a bitch a lesson in manners. I mean, who the hell was he to speak to me like that? To insinuate that Aunt Stevie's funeral wasn't taking the same emotional toll on me as it did his family. Whoever the hell his family was—

"That's him!" Mikey squeals inwardly. *"That's Aunt Stevie's grandson, Jeremy."*

"No fucking way." I breathe aloud in abject horror at Mikey's realization.

Jeremy's face scrunches up some more at my remark. "What? Are you some crazy bitch or something?"

"Watch your mouth there, bruh." Another rumbling, yet familiar voice threatens in that soft menacing way I grew to appreciate in all the years I knew him.

My eyes work overtime to study the tall, dreadlocked guy who became one of my best friends when I moved to Richmond five years ago as a mousey prepubescent girl. His square jaw, tall stature and muscular build made him devastatingly handsome and drew in girls like flies to honey. Oddly, in all the time I'd known him he never dated, but remained the lighthearted playboy bachelor.

"Zay!" Both Mikey and I squeal in delight at the sight of him.

Xavier Rose stops beside me and flashes a friendly grin, revealing stainless white teeth.

"Hey, Von." He greets, sizing up the ginger asshole in front of me. "This guy giving you trouble?"

My cheeks flame instantly by his overprotectiveness, as they always did. "No, Zay. I can handle this. Besides, my friend Jeremy here was just leaving. Right?"

I point the question at Jeremy, whose cheeks have already flushed a darker red than mine from Zay's arrival.

"Right." He mutters, before jetting out of the church. If flustered had a body and face, it would have looked like Jeremy's tall, retreating form as he shuffled through the funeral crowds to find the exit.

Zay pins me with a hard stare. "Von?"

"Yeah, Zay?" I say, returning the serious look he's shooting me.

Out of nowhere, we burst into laughter at what just went down. We're laughing so hard; I'm gripping my sides from the lung pressure of it.

"Did you," Zay wheezed between chuckles, keeling over. "See that look on his face when he ran outta here? He was like," He mirrors the flustered terror that settled on Jeremy's face, bringing a fresh wave of humor to the previously charged tension in the air.

I wince as more laughter assails my body. "Dude! He looked like his mom caught him and was moments from a serious ass whooping or something."

Zay nearly faints into me from the hushed guffaws emanating from his chest. "No, no! I swear he looked more like a tomato. I was about to ask him if his daddy was the ketchup man until he ran out the room."

We both sink onto the empty pew seats, side by side as we recover from the laughter fit the rude boy threw us into. I knew how we appeared, like mean jerks who were throwing jokes at a funeral, but I couldn't help it. Treating people with the same respect they showed to me was just my forte, just as my big brother taught me.

"Dude," I breathe as the last fits of laughter escape me. "What are you doing here? I thought you hated funerals?"

All merriment is drained from his dark skin as he averts his eyes. "Nah, I do. But I remembered last week was the anniversary of Devin's surprise deployment, and that Aunt Stevie's death probably took a huge toll on your emotions and shit. So, now I'm here."

"You are." I mutter, intrigued but grateful for his concern for me. "At the tail-end of the ceremony, too."

He shrugged, a cocky smile on his face. "Yep. I told you, death ain't my thing. But life sure is."

I frowned, confused. "Okay? What's that mean?"

A wry chuckle escapes him as he turns incredulous brown eyes on me. "Don't you remember what today is?"

I wrack my brain, searching all the rooms in the mega Mind Mansion yet again to find meaning. As chatty as Mikey usually is, he does not come to my aid this time.

He reaches over just then to ruffle my wild curls, same as Devin used to do when he was here.

"Hey!" I protest, swatting at him. "Hands off the Do, man."

"Happy birthday, Yvonne." He drawls before pulling me into his arms for the biggest, warmest, bear hug I didn't know I needed.

A stray tear threatens to fall from the unexpected tenderness from my favorite homie, but I blink them away when I catch sight of a warmer pair of green eyes from across the room.

Except, they're not the fiery emerald ones from Jeremy, but the soft and curious ones of a girl with equally red hair. I immediately recognize her as the same girl who helped the older-looking version of her leave the stage when she broke down in the middle of her eulogy. When she notices me noticing her, she jerks her gaze to the floor and rushes out of the room, same as Jeremy.

4

GRAY LIGHT IN A CAVE

My phone vibrates in my back denim pocket, alerting me of a text as I finish off the last of the post-funeral dishes. Even though Mamma Dean owned a dishwasher among several other modern appliances in her seven-bedroom farmhouse, she insisted that dishwashing was a human job, one that ought to be done with sweat and heart. I called that bullshit, but didn't dare share that with her. My gratitude for her hospitality after all these years overshadowed most of the teenage angst I harbored from my old life in DC, the one I often had to coach myself on forgetting.

There are two unread messages I observe in my text inbox. One from Zay, and another from...well, *her*. I shut my eyes tight with rage and dread swarming my chest. I knew I couldn't ignore her forever, but maybe just a little while longer. Besides, it was my birthday, and even though I learned early on in life not to want for anything, to shut off all of my heart's desires no matter how loud they fought to climb to the surface, I couldn't help the desire to shut her out. She made me face the truth. Made me open doors in the mansion I had no business entering. So, steeling myself, I dismissed her text thread and focused on the other one from my favorite homie.

I crinkle my brows as I observe the text message from Zay:

> **ZAY**: That fried chicken Mamma Dean made was good as hell.

I couldn't contain the giggle before texting him back.

> **ME**: Heck yeah, as always.

> **ZAY**: Oh yeah. Stop by my crib later on. I forgot to give you your birthday present.

A present? My mind innocently probed as I considered his words. I appreciated Zay's friendship more than ever, and besides calling each other besties (which he said was much too sissy a title for our relationship) we upgraded ourselves to "favorite homies" shortly after I beat his ass in basketball five years ago.

In all truth, Zay started out as one of Devin's homies when we moved here. It was the most interesting one-eighty, considering my brother existed as a friendless loner back at Easton. I remembered him as constantly stressed out and wound up when we lived in DC, so obsessed with my welfare after what happened to Mikey. Malik Hinton and Bordon Alvarez (who we called Bone) accepted my brother right away (Zay moved to Richmond shortly after we did) when he attended Macon High to finish out his Junior and Senior year of high school and I appreciated that. Gone was the hypervigilant bodyguard, and in its place blossomed my charming older bro, thanks to them. He– no, *we* needed that slice of normal after the hell Lucy the Evil put us through.

Sobering, I briskly tap my response to my favorite homie:

ME: *Lol I'm skeptic, but I'll be there.*

I don't wait for his response when I tiptoe to Mamma Dean's bedroom. No luck. She isn't there. My shoulders sag with the discovery, until intuition tells me to check her beloved lounging area. She and Aunt Stevie, who isn't my or anyone in the community's kin by blood, spent most of their time there between cooking, cleaning and managing the farm. It seemed they spent every ounce of down time together, and my heart swelled in delight as I remembered the echoes of their shared laughter gracing the silent open fields as they chatted.

As assumed, I find her on the back patio, speaking in hushed aggravation with Cousin Dan. Mamma Dean is occupying her same tan rocking chair she usually sits. Except, the twin chair adjacent hers is empty, as Cousin Dan is standing as he exchanges words with Mamma Dean.

Neither of them notice me at the doorway, and judging by the grave expressions on their faces, it feels a disservice to interrupt their back-and-forth. So, I opt for silence.

"She's got to go." Cousin Dan starts. "We can't have them do that to Stevie's house. I don't care if Viv is the legal owner of the property. Stevie wouldn't like this!"

I moisten my suddenly dry lips as I listen for Mamma Dean's response.

"Dan," her tone is weary as she regards the age-old man standing before her. "Don't you think I know that? But what other choice we got?

Like you said, Viv owns the land and the house it sits on. I knew she was only interested in pocketing a profit when she moved down here. When Stevie passed on a week after she and her kids moved in there, I bet she saw nothing but dollar signs."

Cousin Dan's green eyes burn a darker shade of emerald as he spits on the ground. "My sister ain't cold in the ground yet and already she wants to knock it to the ground. Fucking bitch is what she is."

Knock it to the ground? Though I eavesdropped I felt confident in surmising the very worst: Vivian, Aunt Stevie's estranged daughter, is trying to demolish her family home of eighty years. The same home several members of the community and farm gathered for holidays, parties, and plain old communion. Both Mamma Dean and Aunt Stevie's homes were like monumental pillars, known to many travelers and kinfolk alike as a place of rest and warm welcome. Who the hell was this chick? She must be some kind of evil, I gather, to rile up sweet Cousin Dan like that.

The same week the family of three moved in, Aunt Stevie mysteriously died a mere six days after. I pondered the involvement of foul play when I heard my name in the midst of the conversation I half zoned out to.

"Vonnie, come out here. I know you listenin'." Mamma Dean calls out, stilling my heart in its cage.

I crept hesitantly onto the patio, keeping my gaze lowered. "Hey," I say lamely.

Cousin Dan spits, tobacco this time, before saying. "Afternoon, girly."

"Can we help you with something?" Mamma Dean cuts in, still frowning and weary in her funeral clothes.

I fidget with the hem of the white t-shirt I'd since changed into since leaving the funeral. Dresses were never my thing, and I all but bolted to my closet to ditch the "ladylike" frock that clung to parts of my body I preferred hidden. Mamma Dean typically throws a snide comment about my tomboyish attire, but she doesn't so much as glance at the clean white tee and gym shorts I'm sporting. She looks tired.

"Um, yeah." I hedge. "I came to ask if I could go out. To Zay's house."

"I reckon," she answers quickly, waving me away. "But you don't need my permission anymore, young lady. Don't think I forgot. You're eighteen today."

I can't help but furrow my brows at her words. With all the hustle, bustle, and tragedy going on in the wake of her best friend dying mere days ago, I was sure she forgot.

"Of course, she remembers!" Mikey interjects my doubtful thoughts like he usually does, with optimism. *"She loves us."*

I answer him with an eye roll before sputtering. "Right...I'm technically an adult now."

She reared back, her eyes narrowing in suspicion. "Girl, I said you eighteen. Ain't nobody said nothin' bout you being an adult. Long as you live in this house, you still my grandbaby."

"Huh?" I grouse, totally confused by her southern logic again. "You just said I don't need permission anymore."

They both share arid chuckles before she speaks. "You don't, technically. But you need to let me know you leaving and when. I like to know the comings and goings of the people in my house as much as possible. Okay, sweet baby?"

I fight to stifle the eyeroll that desperately wants to reveal itself before nodding. "Right. Sure."

I turn away to begin the twenty-minute trek to the house Zay and his sister share before stopping.

"Can I borrow the truck?"

"I reckon." She clarifies, running a hand through her shoulder length box braid wig. "But only if you give Vivian's kids a tour of the farm like you promised earlier. Okay?"

Damn it, I curse inwardly at our funeral conversation. Of all the things she could have forgotten, why couldn't it have been that? I absolutely seethed at the thought of encountering the ginger asshole again. No way did I predict that going well at all. But my chest does other things when the image of the green-eyed girl resurfaces.

"I just replaced those spark plugs and changed the serpentine belt yesterday morning. Engine should be purring smoother than a kitten on a teat." Cousin Dan...euphemizes in all his redneck glory. It's obvious I've lived on the farm quite a while, because I actually find myself comprehending his message.

"Thanks, Cousin Dan. And I'll be sure to do that, Mamma Dean." I say, fighting hard not to groan the words as I exit the ponderous farmhouse.

I grumble all kinds of expletives as I turn the ignition in the fifteen-year-old Wrangler frequently used by the six farmhands. My journey to driving expertise was rather comical, and I can't resist the grin that spreads across my face as I recall Cousin Dan and Mr. Eddie, Devin's biological dad, teaching me how to operate one of Mamma Dean's old stick shifts. We hadn't lived on the farm more than ten days before Mamma Dean asked I run an errand for her in town to pick up some mulch. I remembered cutting my eyes from side to side, astonished she'd been requesting the youngest face on the farm to operate an actual vehicle.

"Why, here on the farm we teach 'em young to drive." Mamma Dean lamented as she buckled me into the front seat of her bucket truck. "My late husband taught our Eddie to drive when he was no more than eight or nine years old."

As mentioned, I didn't like to use my voice, so Devin speaking in my favor was status quo at that time.

"Respectfully, nah." He huffed. "I do the driving. I don't allow her to do things that ain't safe."

Devin's word was always final when it came to me. Always. So, you can imagine my shock when Mamma Dean shut down the conversation with her syrupy sweet retort.

"Respectfully, you's still a child yourself, grandson. On this farm, chill'un don't make rules and neither are they ever unsafe. Is Vonnie incapable of doing for herself? Don't you have faith in her?"

Now that shut him up and had him mumbling apologies. *My* brother, of all people, was apologizing. However, the impact of her words slammed into me harder than Devin's lack of response on my behalf to the old woman. Not only did I drive myself to the hardware store that day and continued to do so till this very day, but her simple words still rang in my ears: *Don't you have faith in her?* Faith was a foreign concept in my world, and one that surely didn't live in my mansion. I had to add faith to the list under desire of the things I hardened my heart against.

My mind was still reeling over the off-limit virtues of my heart when I caught notice of the small body of water in my peripheral. That small lake just on the edge of the farm technically belonged to Aunt Stevie, but it was just far enough for one to completely disappear into the shroud of darkness when night fell. I went there often, as the silence and frequent noises of nature did wonders to calm the madhouse that lived in my head.

I know I'm close to Zay's house when the town sign appears a little ways ahead. His house, more cabin than house, stood a few feet from the bustle of town, and I smiled as I saw the empty basketball court that shone like a landmark for their

two-bedroom abode. The guys and I balled frequently at Zay's, since his house was the closest to
town and more of a middle ground between all of
our respective houses. His yard was also best suited for the rough and tumble of the games we often played for stakes. Betting was how we bonded
initially, since Devin (who they called DC) and me
moved into town shortly before Zay showed up.
In the beginning, Bone, Malik, and Devin made
up the favorite homie trio, and when Zay and
Shayne moved into the abandoned farmhouse
just off the Carlson Farm they seemed to just fit
right in. As if they were the missing pieces we
truly needed to complete our farm family. Zay,
Bone, and Malik used to work full time for Mamma Dean a couple years ago, but since graduating
high school and entering their twenties, they'd all
gone on to get better paying gigs in the city. Bone
worked at his grandad's mechanic shop fixing
cars all day and Malik just finished trade school
and trained as a barber full time since graduating
last month.

Then there was Zay, who still lived jobless with
his overworked big sister, a nurse who worked
graveyard shifts to cover their expenses. I wondered about their past and dynamic often, since
it was vastly different from mine and Devin's, but

anytime I'd ask Zay about his past, he'd give me a noncommittal shrug and change the subject.

I pulled up and parked the Jeep outside the busted abode, and found myself knocking on the door.

Zay answered, a blunt in his mouth. "Vonnie, what's up?"

"Nothing much, homes." I reply, dapping him before entering the house. We walk through the kitchen and into the living room, where Zay's belongings are laid out. Empty soda cans and Frito bags are sprawled across the cheaply made coffee table, where I also see his PlayStation on pause.

"What you playing?" I asked, pointing to the TV before sitting on the tan sofa.

He smiles brightly. "Man, this that new-new. I just copped the new *Space Mafia* joint."

I gasped. "Shut up!"

He nods, before plopping down next to me on the couch. He takes a long drag from his blunt before passing it to me. "Hell yeah. Just got it last week. Been playing it all morning. Cost me a grip to get it early, too."

"I bet." I say, choking on the blunt he just passed me. "Let me play you."

He yawns, nodding toward the controller on the table. "Go ahead. Show them alien motherfuckers wassup."

Boy, do I. Even though I'd only ever fangirled this game on social media and stalked its next month's release, I navigated the controls and intergalactic dimensions with ease. I end up defeating Forkin Cobslauter, the alien overlord and don of the Cobslauter Crime Family who'd been terrorizing my home planet. His mafia had been stealing girls from my planet, Mars, where the girls are more fertile and gullible enough to be used in matters of intergalactic trade.

"Damn, Von!" Zay whistled his approval as he watched the screen. About an hour or so went by and I didn't even notice it as I reentered Mars. "You almost finished the game. Damn!"

I pause, and lay the controller sheepishly onto the coffee table. "Sorry, man. I didn't even know all that time had passed. My bad..."

I just noticed his attire, and he's wearing a tattered Wu Tang tee shirt and black sweat pants that make him look sort of homeless, and I wonder how he found the cash to afford this game on pre-release.

I open my mouth to ask him just that, when he holds a hand up to pause my words.

"Hold up!" He coughs, after placing the blunt in the ashtray and running down the hall toward his bedroom. The hell?

He returns with a white grocery bag, a Food Lion bag Virginians called it, and tosses it at me.

I dodge it like a bomb. "Ew, what's this?"

He glares at me before sitting back down on the couch. "Man, open the damn bag and shut the fuck up."

I roll my eyes, and reach for the item I hoped wouldn't be gross.

My eyes bug at what I uncover.

"Xavier!" I scream before throwing myself at him.

"Von!" He chokes under my unyielding arms around his neck. "Happy...birthday...can't breathe."

"Sorry," I uttered apologetically before resetting myself back to neutrality. I had to keep calm, I reminded myself, but this gift was...just too much. Too damn thoughtful to be coming from a son of bitch like him. A broke son of a bitch at that.

"Zay, do you know what this is?" I asked, knowing he wasn't too keen on war games like I was.

He chuckles, a boyish grin on his face before responding. "Hell yeah, I do. I got it for you when

I went to pick up *Space Mafia* in town. I know it's your favorite game."

A tear rolls down my eye on its own accord, and I rush to wipe it before he sees.

"Aw, no, don't cry, Von. It's slight work. It's no big deal."

"It's *Weapons from Zeldar 4*, Zay! This is like...the best gift ever. Shit, I need to get home so I can play this." I'm blubbering by the time I stand up with the goods in my hands.

He stands, too. "Yeah, and remind me not to let you hit the blunt before getting gifts again."

I punch him on the arm. "Whatever!"

We're giggling like schoolgirls as we walk through the kitchen to the backyard where my truck is. Zay always made it a habit to walk me to my truck, no matter the time of day, insisting that it's 'what my big bro would want' if he were there. I've since stopped protesting the kind gesture.

A black Honda pulls up just then, parking right beside my truck. I needed to return to the farm before it got too late. I recognize Shay Rose, Zay's older sister, instantly in her light pink scrubs and high braid bun. She'd gotten a little thicker since she'd first moved here a few years ago, and that only seemed to add to her overall beauty, in my opinion.

"Vonnie?" She calls incredulously as she exits the driver side of the car. She's carrying a fast-food bag in her hands. "Hey, sweetie. Where you been at?"

I smiled at her, willing the evening breeze to sober me up enough to make the drive back home. "Hi, Shay! Sorry about that. I've been working the farm and chilling mostly. I'll try to visit more often."

"Good, oh and happy birthday! Zay reminded me that it was your special day the other day. Sorry I didn't get you anything…"

"It's okay, really!" I say.

Her face brightens. "Oh, I know! Stop by sometime later on and I'll bake you something. I know cakes are played out, so just let me know what you like and I'll make it. Okay?"

My insides warmed at the thought of eating one of Shay's desserts. Her sweets were widely regarded as top tier from all over the farm. I couldn't pass that up, birthday or not.

I climb into my truck, but keep the door open as I shout, "Thanks, Shay. I'll take you up on that."

"Great!" She muses, then her face falls a bit at her next question. "You haven't heard from Devin, have you?"

Ah, fuck. I knew she'd ask about the brother I'd only heard through rumor that she dated.

I gulp. "No. He hasn't said anything to me."

Zay clears his throat. "And that's enough questions for the birthday girl. See you this weekend for ball?"

I nod, grateful for the conversation pivot. "I'll be here."

"All right." Shay grumbles petulantly as she walks to the door. "No betting or gambling, Zay. I don't want to hear no shit about you owing somebody some money again. *Capisce?*"

He rolls his eyes, shutting my car door. "Yeah, yeah, all right. I hear you, no bets."

"I mean it!" She squeals. "Don't make me kick your ass out of here."

"Shay!" He barks, but I don't hear the rest of the argument as I ease the truck in reverse out of the yard.

I'm a little high, so I make it a point to roll the window down and let the air in as I drive. There's little on my mind as I make the short drive back to Carlson Farms, but I'm super excited about playing my new game when I get back to my room. I look outside and take in the beautiful scenery and the calm quiet of the lake just off the farm. A chill evening on the lake sounds like just the thing I need. Besides, I smell a little too much like weed for my liking, and I groan at the thought of entering the house to Mamma Dean's interrogation of why I 'smell like the devil's been busy.' Yeah, I think, I'll just take a quick detour and bask in the solitude of the lake. I hated to swim...hated it for reasons I didn't dare dredge up, so I know I won't swim or anything. Just a little chill sesh is all I need to get the weed out of my clothes.

Resolving myself, I make a sharp turn in the dirt road connecting into town and branch off into the rocky terrain of the trees. I make it as far as the water's edge, however, before catching sight of something red floating on the lake's surface.

"Maybe it's a duck?" Mikey surmises, and I'm trembling with fear at the unknown at that point.

Too stunned to answer my eerily optimistic brother.

I tip toe on frozen feet to the normally tranquil waters, my heart a chunk of ice in my chest for fear of the worst. The cloud of red leads me to believe against Mikey's duck idea, as I'm sure the source of this red cloud is human.

"N-No...!" I shriek in mute terror and fall to my knees when I witness the sight: Her fiery red hair and ghost-pale face confirms the identity of the girl floating lifelessly before me. What did Mikey say her name was again?

It's Kimberly! He screams in answer to my inward panicky questions I'm not quite sure were meant for him. I feel my eyes roll back as the sight of her lifeless body, drifting rather peacefully, plunges me back in time.

5

LIVING ROOM

I hold my breath to resist the urge to inhale t*he invading fluid in my lungs. Screams fill the air around me, but the sound is muffled due to my ears being submerged in water. Except, no, it isn't water. As I open my mouth to scream out for help, I know it's useless, but I do it anyway because even in this dire situation hope still lived in me. But I taste and ingest the bitter fluid that threatens to suffocate my small lungs. The fluid, I learned a lot later, is not water, but kerosene.*

I force my head up, begging the blunt force pushing my head into the fluid to rejoin the land of barely living. Every muscle in my body throbs from the exertion of fighting: fighting the man who forced me into this bathtub. Fighting the infernal fluid threatening to overtake me. Overall, I'm fighting for the will to see her again. I've got to get to her, know she's safe. I don't immediately remember how I got here or how the man's hand ends up plunging my head into this pungent liquid, but I am sure of one huge thing. I've got to help her. Even though I'm screaming under all of this fluid, I know she isn't. She never does. She doesn't use her voice, and I'm sure that as long as I can lift my head just high enough I can be her sound. I can be the beautiful voice she decides against using in spite of the failing lungs in my chest. Perhaps I can be a distraction so that she can get away. Go far from this underground hell and run, scream, even plead for a haven. We've never had one of those, and it's something I'd always wanted. The three of us together in harmony, but I know I'll never make it out of here. I know as sure as the day is bright and the dark breeds night that my finite fate and future will soon be decided. My heart aches alongside the stabbing pains in my lungs at the thought of not being there to protect her anymore, my voiceless angel and twin. Just give me some air, I scream in submergence and thrash against the meaty arm holding me under. Let me at least call her, make sure she knows to run and let my voice be the beacon. Find a haven that leads to home.

"Just fucking go still already!" An accented dark voice rumbles above me.

I feel his hands wrap around my throat just as I feel her fear rising. I know it. Her heart is racing in agonizing desperation for my welfare, but I'm glad it's beating. Mine won't, and I know it won't all too soon but I can't resist the urge to be her hero one more time. Be the voice of my twin flame if only to call her name. While I knew this maneuver would mean my death, fear became the farthest emotion from my collapsing organs as I bit into his hand and rose out of the water. I needed to speak, to call her name to remind her of her new purpose, to run away and find a haven. Coppery blood filled my mouth, his blood, and I grit my teeth with new resolve before doing the unthinkable. In the underground hell where our worlds fell apart, I rose from the tub and hollered her name.

"Yvonne!" My throat burns from the strain of my own voice and the mix of kerosene and blood awash in my mouth.

It hurts. Damn it, it hurts. But I try my voice again, praying inside it reaches wherever she is in the insipid darkness of the underground room. Find a haven! Find a home! I don't have the strength to yell those words aloud, but manage out her name one final time before the hands return around my neck to fill the empty silence with snapping and popping noises— the noises that come from breaking bone under extreme pressure. One more time, I coached myself in my final living second before calling out to her again. Just one...more...time...!

"Yvonne?!" A voice calls out. I don't quite know where I am or what time it is, but the persistent urgency in who I assume to be a lady's voice brings immediate panic to my heart and mind. Just what the fuck happened? I'd been asleep most of the day, and could only vaguely recall some moments from before. The funeral conversation, my birthday, no, our birthday, Zay, the redheaded rude dude, then–

"Yvonne!" The girl calls again, shaking me this time so that I come awake to the world again in her thin, cold arms.

"Yvonne? That's your name, isn't it?" The redheaded girl's panicked face comes into focus just then, and for a moment...everything stops.

The hums of nature around the lake that bring with it birdsong and the occasional howl in the distance don't dare register as my eyes connect with her green ones. I can't resist the pull to touch her for real, like I'd been secretly wanting to when I first seen her come into town last week.

Without a second thought, my hand cups her cheek. "Kimberly...is that you? That your name?" I rasp.

Her cheeks burn from our contact, and I sense the previous concern waning a degree as she sputters, "U-Um, yes. Are you all right? When I finished my swim I heard a scream and saw you unconscious on the ground here..."

A slow smile spreads across my face and I'm...warm all of a sudden. I use the hand pressed against her face to feel her forehead. Then her ears. Then her nose.

She jerks away from me when I begin to run my finger along the outline of her lips and I groan as the move thrusts me to the hard ground.

She's kneeling over me again with renewed worry. "Oh, no! I didn't mean to push you like that! Sorry...it's just you started touching me and made me uncomfortable."

"Kimberly." I rasp again, and the resonance of my voice weirds me out a bit as I study her again. "Can you just...lay with me?"

She's kneeling still as she regards my weak body lying flat on its back. The sun that was previously shining bright in the sky is now giving way to an evening dusk. The crickets' song replaces the morning birds' and I'm oddly compelled to just be beside her. The hesitation and confusion from before when we locked eyes in the funeral is gone, and I just crave to be real. Real with her, even if it's for a little while. I extend my hand out to her with an anxious heart filling with hope.

After a long minute passes, she gingerly lays beside me without ever taking my hand.

"I'll lay here with you, if that's what you want." She drawls in that weird mix of southern and northern like her mother spoke. "But I won't touch you. I don't do that. Ask anybody that knows me."

I nod in spite of the disappointment and sadness filling my chest. I wonder about the experiences she's lived through to come to a decision like that, but think again. If I ask her about her demons, she'd want to know about mine, and I couldn't dredge those up. No, I didn't want to dredge them up for fear of the Mind Mansion. It had a way of pulling me into rooms I desperately needed staying shut.

"Kimmy." She states. A tranquil look graces her delicate features and my heart stutters when she pins those dark greens on me. "My friends call me Kimmy. It's nice finally meeting you, neighbor."

Instead of voicing one of those questions, I responded to one of her earlier more panicked inquiries.

"I'm Michael." I respond evenly and finish off despite the confused look she casts me. "But my friends and fam call me Mikey."

6

STAY AWHILE, MY LOVE

Soft lips crash against mine and before long I'm squirming and burning from the rush of sensation jolting through me. Those hands run the length of my bare back and the unrelenting feathery touch makes me purr in delight. *So good*, I thought dreamily as the figure continued their delicious conquest of my body. I part my thighs to allow them further access to explore my tenderest parts, and for once my mind is at total peace with my body's actions.

"We shouldn't," the figure with a voice like molten honey says.

An eerie semblance of familiarity snakes its way into my mind but not before I find myself responding to that protest.

"Hey, hey. You're in control." I hear myself say. "I can barely breathe at the sight of you, you're so damn beautiful, but please trust me. I don't want you to do anything you'll regret, so..."

I wait for the familiar pink to color my cheeks at the bold words I'd never speak to somehow make their way past my lips.

I can't see what's unfolding, but my mind's eye is clear as I take a seat at the front row and feel the sensations.

"Thank you." the figure whispers before something prods at my opening.

I howl at the unexpected pleasure that rockets through my being.

"Thank you," the figure repeats as another wave of desire crashes into my writhing body. There's so much pleasure it's hard to think clearly, hard to reason with the incongruousness of the situation. I should be questioning all sorts of things, like where I was or who was that but I only arch my body and whimper for more of her touch instead.

Tides of desire ride the waves of my writhing, prone body and I'm barely able to register rhyme or reason at that point. Four walls surround me and I realize I'm peering through a window to experience the delicious joy of being in her arms.

Her arms.

No, more like fingers.

Her fingers pierce my lower heat, and I moan at the sensation caused by her now drenched digits.

"I see you." She whispers, so low I almost think I imagined it.

"Mmm." Is all I can manage out at this point as the crest of something big threatens to overtake me. I'm so close...so close to the edge I can almost—

Two large eyes stare directly through the window, and I blanche from fear. I'm still riding the wings of the climax as cold rationale assails me.

Four walls.

A window.

Those large green eyes.

Oh, fuck no! No, no, no! I'm in a room. One of the rooms of the goddamn Mind Mansion and I can't begin to understand how I ended up here. Was it an emergency? Did something happen? And if so, where was Mikey?

I turn away from those large green eyes that somehow penetrated the mansion to gauge my little brother's presence. He was there. And unharmed, but I wasn't quite sure what he was doing. Just before I open my mouth to connect with my twin brother, her voice rings out through my mind again.

"I see you. I feel you." There's a desperate urgency in her voice I kind of recognize. "Tell me you feel me, too."

"I do!" My voice answers, shocking me in place. "Give me a piece of you. Let me know this is real..."

I wake up in a cold sweat just then. The air is tense as the thick cloud of heat encircling my bed and sweaty body as I study my whereabouts. A room. My room. After palming my chest, I realized I was still dressed in the same tee and gym shorts from earlier, but I did not recall exactly how I ended up back at Mamma Dean's. Frustrated, I slapped my face to force recognition to the surface. The more I searched my mind for reason the more I knew, and the more I dreaded the truth. Fuck. I lost time again. Except...

"Mikey?" I gently beckoned my brother aloud. Silence.

Shaking myself to gather my wits, I cleared my throat and called for my brother. Except, there was only a resounding silence echoing in the halls of the mansion. I...felt him. Yes, he was there, but it was almost like he was asleep somehow.

"Mikey!" I said, my voice now a trembling groan.

"Vonnie?" He answered, sending waves of relief through my heart. *"Sis? That you?"*

I wipe the tear I didn't realize fell down my cheek and nod. *"Yes! Bro, where were you?"*

"I..." His voice wavers a bit, as if he's still on screen but not quite on the right channel. *"I don't know what that was. Did you, um...were you there for that?"*

"There for what—" I almost ask, but the memory of her fingers in my core revitalizes my latent anger towards him. *"Mikey! What the hell happened? Did you take over? All I remember is driving from Zay's house and then bam— I woke up here."*

I wait for the carefully curated response from my levelheaded brother, but it never comes. Great, I harumph, giving me the good ol' silent treatment. I want to give him some more hell for taking over and not filling me in on the details, but something tells me to back off. I'm almost tempted to reach for his journal, the one he keeps whenever he takes over has any lucid enough moments in which he needs to write down his thoughts. Our agreement was solid, I thought, chewing on my lip as I regarded the green composition book that housed my dead brother's innermost feelings.

He was to never take over unless due to emergency, and in return his diary was purely off-limits. This deal kept the ship running smoothly over the years, and I'm a little terrified to think of this new rift that caused him to go completely rogue.

He'll reveal it to me in time, I intuit before grabbing my cell phone from my pocket.

One text, as I figured, from Zay asking me to let him know when I got home. I know he was probably worried that I left super high to operate a vehicle. Guilt roils through me at missing his text, but fear chases those feelings down when I peek at the messages from...her.

HER: *You can't keep avoiding me, Von.*

I delete the thread, per usual, and shut my eyes to keep the visions of the past at bay.

Sleep soon claims me, and I welcome it with a fatigue that chased me since that hauntingly erotic dream.

7

DON'T SPEAK

"Shoot, bitch!" ErnestoCrestOH! screams through my headset as I hurriedly navigate with the overused controller. After a few more fumbles with the pesky buttons, I'm finally able to destroy the invading alien that's infiltrated our barracks.

"Finally, *CasaRaptor7*." He sighs my screen name in relief. "Thought that alien had you for a second."

I roll my eyes, a smug smile on my face. "Ye of little faith, bro. Employ the cleanup crew. This ship's got to be tip top before we ride out to StinsGar Realm on Zeldar."

He chuckles. "Aye, aye, sir. I'm on it."

Warmth crashes through me as I study the crew dutifully obeying my orders. In this world, I was king. I was respected. I had an excellent group of online comrades who understood my love of gaming perfectly. Even though I graduated high school last month, gaming still felt like the perfect after school activity to get me through a rainy day. *Weapons from Zeldar* was my favorite game as of late, and I'd probably played it fifteen times since its inception four years ago. I decided to replay games one through three in order to get the full effect of the game Zay gifted me. The mere thought of that precious gem still made me teary eyed as I poise my space gun at another alien intruder.

"Vonnie Elizabeth Carlson!" I hear a faint voice yell beyond me. My virtual comrades, like *ErnestoCrestOH!* did not have enough personal information to refer to me by my government name. My heart flutters as I look up to the source of the noise and groan.

Mamma Dean is standing at the door frame tapping her toe and glaring at me.

"Hang on, ErnestoCrestOH!" I yank off the headphones and stare over at her. "Hey, Mamma Dean. What's up?"

"What's up?" She mocks incredulously, like I'm the dumbest bitch on the planet or something.

I clear my throat and try again. "Um, okay. How's it hanging?"

"Yvonne!" She grits.

"Yes, ma'am?" I learned early on to tack on the *ma'am* for every situation.

She stomps inside my room to loom over my seated form on my beanbag chair. "Didn't I ask you to give those kids a tour?"

I purse my lips, wincing. "Yikes. Uh. No?"

"Then why is Viv calling me saying Kimmy told her she never got that tour, huh? Didn't I ask you kindly?"

I'm still wincing. "Yes. Sorry, Mamma Dean. But, do they really need the tour? Haven't they visited before?"

"If you maybe listen when I speak, you'd remember me tellin you that they've never been here before, and they only met Stevie on her dying day. Stevie promised to escort them around the land and…never got a chance to do that."

She choked on the last part, and I allowed the guilt to wash over me then. The raw pain on her face made me feel like the largest asshole on the face of Richmond, and I steeled myself for whatever happened next. I was an adult now and Mamma Dean reassured both Devin and I upon moving here that she didn't do physical discipline. She only told us that after Devin divulged some of what happened in DC, and only after she bore witness to the puckered skin on his right shoulder where Lucy's bullet grazed him.

I found myself bracing whenever she or Mr. Eddie, Devin's biological dad, entered a room.

"Hey, girl." Mr. Eddie sat me down one morning at breakfast time before he went to work the fields. "I ain't your daddy, so I have no business telling you right from wrong. I do have a strict set of rules I set for myself, however."

I stared at him with wide-eyed curiosity and caution. I never responded. Didn't use my voice, and made myself small to get through the interaction like I typically did whenever Lucy the Evil's male friends addressed or undressed me with their eyes.

I squeezed my eyes shut, fearing whatever Mr. Eddie would make me do to leave the room. What kind of favor would it be?

"Look at me, Yvonne." He said gently from across the table.

I did, and saw him with his fists in the air. "I don't know all of what y'all went through from before, but understand that you'll never be hurt here. At least not physically. Lemme know you understand."

I bobbed my head up and down in agreement.

He nodded once. "Good. Now, if in the event you find yourself wanting to shrink away from somebody. Or if you feel threatened in any way. Follow these rules: raise your dukes. Go on."

I gingerly raised my balled hands to mimic his.

"That's right. These are your greatest weapons. If the threat is taller than you, use the heel of your hand to strike his chin. Do whatever you got to do to get away, and find me, or Devin, or anybody else on the farm you trust to handle it. Okay?"

A slow smile spread across my face as I recalled one of the first men I truly trusted. Mr. Eddie owned the same spirit as Devin, fiercely loyal and protective of those they loved, and I loved them both for it. I hadn't braced myself since that day, hadn't felt the threat of attack like I usually did when my mind automatically went on autopilot and lost me time.

So, the recoil took me by surprise as I regarded Mamma Dean standing before me.

I stood up. "I'm sorry, Mamma Dean. I know it's been really hard for you since Aunt Stevie's passing. I didn't mean to disobey or make your life harder in any way. I'll go right now, okay?"

She nodded, extending her arms out to me. I walked into them and hugged her with all my might.

"No, no." She sniffled. "I'm sorry. Lord, if I had known losing Stevie would hurt this bad, I'd have brought some whiskey to that funeral."

I shook my head, caressing her back as I spoke. "Mamma Dean. That's not the way to deal. Come on now, what would Devin say? Or Eddie?"

"I'm just messing." She chuckled, both of us aware of her twenty-year oath to sobriety. "Maybe you can teach me how to play one of those video games of yours. What's that, Star Wars?"

I laughed, parting from the hug to look at her. "Mamma Dean! It's not Star Wars, it's *Weapons from Zeldar.*"

"Well, whatever it is, show me how it's done sometime, okay? If you find it important, then so do I."

I hugged her tight again before saying, "I love you, granny."

"Love you, Vonnie." She sighed. "Now get over to Stevie's—I mean, Viv's house. Supper will be done soon."

"Okay," I mumble before donning a light jacket and mini denim shorts. An odd combo, I know, but the September breeze was becoming a little cooler each day as the sun set.

I didn't ask permission this time to borrow the truck since it was available in the lot. The drive to Aunt Stevie's was brisk, since she lived just a mile off Carlson Farms.

My heart thudded at the prospect of seeing this family again. Last I checked, Jeremy was just a dick who had it out for me, and Kimberly...

The dream comes back to me as I park the truck in front of the huge farmhouse. I'm panting at the memory of her hands wandering up and down my body and my pussy dripping from her intrusion.

Kimmy... I hear Mikey's voice in the recesses of my mind hum her name, like a prayer.

Why does the thought of her do this to me? Send me into the strangest of fantasies? Each time I try to speak to Mikey about it, he goes silent, disappearing into one of those unexplored rooms in my mind.

Get it together, Von. I tell myself as I climb out of the truck. Mamma Dean was hyper fixating on giving these people the grand tour, so if that's what she wanted, I'd do it. No matter how stupid I deemed the task.

I noticed that only the screen door was used instead of the heavy wooden one. Instinctively,

I pushed through the flimsy barrier and entered the dark house.

It was so dark inside I almost turned and exited under the assumption that nobody was home. Maybe Mamma Dean got it wrong, I thought, because not a peep of sound or any other indicator of life could be detected within the shadows. No parts of Aunt Stevie's house had been touched or moved, and Cousin Dan's words came back to me, confusing me all the more. If Vivian was bulldozing the place, it didn't look like it, as she threw none of Aunt Stevie's belongings out, much less touched anything. It looked like Aunt Stevie was simply in another room instead of another world.

Readying myself to leave, I turned around. The faintest of voices, and I mean super faint, could be heard from upstairs. I crane my neck to listen more intently to the small voice, and familiarity hits me as I creep closer to the sound.

It's Kimmy.

But who is she talking to? I wonder this as I ascend the long wooden steps. I tiptoe, though it's to no avail since the wooden floors creak under my weight and act as an echolocation to my coordinates. I almost feel like one of those black ops spies from that espionage video game I played all

last year, called *Killer Silence*. The badass heroine always got the gold she thefted, but I felt more like Vonnie the Clutz as another squeal whined from the floorboards.

I can make out what she's saying as I'm now outside the door of what I assume to be her bedroom. The room was one of Aunt Stevie's game rooms when she was alive.

"Heath," Kimmy says, almost pleadingly. "Please leave us alone. We were only playing Tea Party. Let us play in peace."

There's no response from whoever this Heath guy is, and it makes me think she's on the phone.

Suddenly, a cold burst of air rushed through the room, chilling my bones and making me shiver on contact.

"Hey!" Kimmy yells. "I mean it! She's your daughter for Christ sake, let her have some fun! Get away from this house. You aren't welcome here."

Fear creeps its way through my body as I listen to the one-sided conversation. While the temperature was changing outside, a gust that cold was really out of place. For all intents and purposes, it was still summery outside.

"I don't like this, Vonnie." Mikey's voice manifests, scaring the shit out of me.

I jump. *"Mikey! Where've you been?"*

He continues, ignoring my question. *"Vonnie, please check on her. Go inside. She might be in danger."*

"But, Mike—"

"Go!" the word leaves my mouth, but it isn't my own. It's Mikey.

The floor quakes and I yelp, "Holy shit!" before hopping inside the bedroom.

I scan the room for her, for Kimmy, and to my relief, she's sitting at a small white table. Stuffed bears occupy the small toddler seats and there is an entire tea spread on the table.

Kimmy is dressed in a frilly white, wedding style dress.

"K-Kimmy?" I hedge, getting closer to her. She looks up, but what I see in her eyes almost makes me run away. Her eyes are pure white where they're typically emerald, as if they're rolled to the back of her head. My heart thunders as I gulp and repeat, "Kimmy?"

"Jenna?" She probes softly, looking around the room, but not really seeing me, I guessed.

I sat beside her, shoving one of the stuffed animals to the floor and stealing its seat. I wrap my hand over hers. "Hey, stay with me! Do you need to go to the hospital? Are you in trouble?"

A moment passes, and three words come to me then, and in that moment I knew in my heart to repeat them to her, like she did me.

"I see you." I say, repeating her words to me from the dreams. "I see you. Come back, Kimmy. Tell me how to help."

She shut her eyes and shakes her head violently from side to side. She's shaking so hard I have to subdue her arms down.

Tears roll down her eyes as she suddenly pauses. The cold wind is gone, and the temperature returns to normal.

Her eyes open to reveal the usual emeralds, causing both Mikey and me to sigh in relief. "Michael?" She whispers, looking me in the eyes. "No, you're Yvonne. Yvonne! Where am I?"

I frown, glancing around the poorly decorated room with a single twin bed. "You're in Aunt Stevie's house. You're home."

She shakes her head, wincing. "No, this isn't home. Too many...too many bad spirits here."

"Bad spirits?" I ask, still holding her. "What do you mean, bad spirits? And why did you...why did you call me Michael?"

She sits up as if waking from a dream and frees herself from my arms. She averts her guilty eyes away.

"I feel like..." she starts nervously. "I feel like I can trust you with this. You deserve to know."

"Know what?" I demand, concern, confusion and anger swirling through me. "Tell me now! Why was the room so cold? And you calling me, Michael...just who are you?"

"Yvonne, I..."

"Who?!" I screeched, more than a little freaked out.

"I see ghosts!" She bellowed, tears still streaming. "I see them all the time. Spirits I call them. That's how I know Michael. He introduced himself to me the other day when you fainted. We sort of...um..."

I reach to grab her hand, when the memory of her admission floats back. She didn't like to be touched. I stood up instead, retreating.

"No." I whispered in horror. "Stop it. You're just some psycho who came here to fuck with me. Just stop it—"

"No!" She defended, standing and meeting me. "Yvonne...it's me, remember?"

I stared at her, the desperation in her tone forcing me to reenter the rooms in my mind to search for meaning again.

"It's true, Von. Mikey corroborated inwardly. *We did meet. We spoke and..."*

"Mikey!" I bellowed angrily, not caring at this point if the ghost girl thought I was the crazy one.

I pinned accusatory eyes on her. "What did you do, huh? What happened to my brother? Are you the reason he barely speaks to me lately?"

She averts her eyes again, gnawing on her lip before nodding. "Yvonne, we...Michael and I were...together. Me and you were together. By the lake...please try to remember. Gosh, I'm so stupid!"

"Just let her speak, Vonnie. Let her explain."

"Why, Mikey? I'm mad at you, too. You had sex with this girl without me knowing? That's violating on a whole other level. And just plain creepy!"

The next words he whispered in my mind made my jaw drop.

"I love her, Vonnie! Please, just hear her out. For me. Okay?"

8

MEMENTO MORI

I could stand there and hear her out, I rationalize as I stare at the frantic redhead before me in a white dress, but I just don't want to. I really, really, didn't want to groom any more of this madness from spinning out of control. This girl needed meds, and while I wasn't a pillar of sanity nor the final judge on it, I knew she needed help beyond my expertise.

And I needed to get out of there.

"Vonnie," Mikey warned, *"did you hear me? I told you I'm in love with her. Please don't leave her alone right now."*

"Mikey, no excuse me, Michael, since that's what she calls you, this is madness. You can't love her."

"Why not?"

I roll my eyes. *"Because, you don't know what love is. You're too young. And you've barely met her!"*

"Don't know what love is?" He countered dryly. *"I love you. I know that. And I know you know that. Plus, I'm just as old as you. I'm an eighteen-year-old man, Von. Put some respect on me, man."*

"You want to talk about respect?!" I nearly shout, appalled by his audacity. "You fucked a whole person without me present. That sounding *respectful* to you?"

Kimmy's hand shoots out, and they're ice cold and trembling as she caresses me.

"Please, don't blame him, Yvonne. He offered to stop at any given point, but I...I wanted it to happen. I can't explain why I feel this connection with you, but just understand that I'm the one to blame. Not your brother."

I'm puzzled, but only for a moment, at her words. At her lame apologies. But then I realize I voiced that last retort out loud.

I yank my arm away from her and try to ignore the guilt that rises from the hurt expression on her face at my actions.

"I deserved that." She muttered sullenly.

I take a deep, steadying breath. "Okay. Okay. Here's how this is gonna go."

She shoots me a hopeful look. "I'll do anything to make this up. I didn't mean to cause a rift between you both. Or violate your body in any way...I understand what that's like...having someone touch you without permission or knowledge of consent."

Warm fuzzies make their way past my stone clad heart at her words and willingness to believe in Mikey's existence. It was refreshing to speak with someone who didn't question the validity of his presence in my mind or the state of my sanity. I'm also angered and saddened by the latter part of her admission.

I collapse into one of the mini chairs again. "I'll give you what you want, but only if you give me what I want."

A frown furrows her scarlet brows. "You want to give me something?"

"Not give you, Kimmy. Bargain."

"A bargain?" A look of terror crinkles her face for a moment. "What do you want?"

"Nothing like that. I'll give you what you deserve in all this."

Her pale face blanks.

I sigh. "Blame. I'm blaming you for all of it. For taking advantage of me, my brother, and my body. That's all on you to deal with. Take it up with your god for punishment, or your therapist. It's not my deal."

Her jaw flexes as she retreats an unconscious step. "Okay."

"Okay," I parrot, resigned. "In return, you let me give you this dumbass tour of the farm my crazy grandma won't let me get out of. You and Jeremy."

"Jeremy? As in, my younger brother Jeremy?" She asks.

"Um, yeah. That gonna be a problem?"

"Take it easy on her, Von." Mikey scolds. I ignore him, of course, as his input in any of this really doesn't matter at this point. We needed to read-just our borders and boundaries, as this recent incident existed way outside the parameters of plain old wrong.

"I'm fine, Michael." Kimmy responds absent-ly, then adds, "I agree. I'll do this for you. Even though I've explored the grounds of Carlson Farms and Grandma Stevie's property, I'll do whatever to make this up. Okay?"

I flinch. "Wait. You heard what Mikey just said?"

"W-What?" She glanced guilty away, blushing. "I didn't hear anything."

I stood up, straightened and hovered close to her, but not touching. "A minute ago, you could see ghosts, now you wanna lie about it?"

"I'm sorry, Yvonne. I want to be honest with you, but—"

"But what?"

"I'm just a little too used to being called crazy. Of being the frightening, friendless, outcast. I couldn't, um, bare it if you saw me the same way. I don't want you to call me...crazy. Gosh, how dumb must I sound!"

I sucked in a quick breath, unable to handle the emotion building in my heart. I hate this. I hate how much I want to hate ghost girl but can't. If anything, I resonated with her on a new level, and it's not sympathy that haunts me as I stare at her, but a newfound respect and adoration. I want to comfort her. I want to gather the scarred girl in my arms like Devin would do me whenever I had a bad dream. Fear grips my heart at the realization that it was me, Yvonne Carlson, who wanted to be the source of comfort and protector against all the ghosts that threatened this beautiful soul. I saw her. Like she saw me, in that moment, and I clench my fists to keep from acting on that desire to embrace her.

"I don't think you're crazy. Not even close." I grumble, my voice coming out harder than intended to force the tears at bay.

A small smile tugs her lips upward and I damn near swoon at the image she created. Fucking beautiful was what she was.

"Then that's a relief. Thank you. Both of you."

Mikey vibrates inside my head from the acknowledgements and gratitudes, and I almost shimmy with him until a thought comes.

"So, you can hear Mikey. That's established. Creepy for me, but at least it's a known. Now, where is your brother?"

She frowned, considering it. "I think he said he was going to the gym or something. He should be back soon if you want to wait here with me…"

I shook my head, mostly to convince myself that the idea wasn't the most horrible. "Nope. We'll go get him. I know exactly what gym he's at."

"You do?" She asked, following me down the stairs. We're almost to the car when she adds, "why do you know where he is?"

I chuckled as I entered the truck. "Because Builds and Guilds Gym is the only one in town at a walkable distance from the farm. Get in."

"Right!" She acquiesced before climbing into the old Jeep.

We make the drive in complete silence, not an awkward one, but thoughtful. I consider all the craziness unfolding in my otherwise stable home life right now and grimace. My routine existed daily as waking up, gaming, running errands in town for the farmhands, balling on the weekends and...gaming some more. Lackluster, I knew, but there was a time in my life where all I craved was boredom, consistency, and just one day I wasn't living in fear. I often wake up to visions of Lucy at my door in the middle of the night, a cigarette in her hand as she wakes me and asks me to do her a "favor." All things from that old life were mostly replaced with good memories here on the farm, with my makeshift farm family and an accepted spot in the Carlson crew. Since the adoption was finalized three years ago, both me and Devin were official Carlson's. Honorary Carlson's with purpose, friends, and a home we could be proud of instead of a house we cowered inside with fear. This mind play since Kimmy's family arrived was...what did Mikey call it...triggering the fuck out of me. And I needed to set things back to the normal I needed, the home we fought for in order to get a grip of life again.

"How old are you?" I find myself asking her.

She clears her throat. "Um, I turned twenty-two, two days ago."

I nearly swerved the truck into oncoming traffic at her admission. "What? Your birthday was...two days ago?"

She nods, suspicious. "Yes...why?"

I don't mention to her that we shared the same birthday for fear of connecting with her. I can't connect with her. She was off limits. The enemy. The interloper here to destroy my home and happiness. Right?

"Why'd they schedule your grandmother's funeral on your birthday? That's a little fucked, isn't it?"

Kimmy purses her lips, her eyes falling. "Yeah. I know."

Hating the tension in the air, I change the subject. "You know, you don't look a day over eighteen."

She laughs, a throaty song that pierces my insides. "Oh, why, thanks. Same to you. If I had to guess, I'd say you've not aged a day over eighteen, either."

I smirk, in spite of myself. "Well, then you'd guess right, darlin."

"What?" She yips. "You're really eighteen years old?"

"Yup."

"That's...all?"

"Uh, yeah. Now it's my turn to ask. Why is that so shocking?"

She cupped regretful hands to her face. "Gosh, I really am a perv. You're just an eighteen-year-old kid. And I...had sex with you."

I'm not sure why her anguish and regret makes me feel challenged and mildly hurt, but it does. I turn to her as I nearly drive by what I know is Zay's house before we hit the town sign. "I'm not a kid. And while I wasn't exactly in the room when we fucked, I remembered you enjoyed my fingers in your pussy same as I did yours. We had adult fun, okay?"

"Gosh..." she breathes abashedly. "Do you have to say it like that? *Fucked* is such a gritty way to put...what we did by the lake."

Now that makes me laugh. Hard.

"What's so funny?" She half laughs as I wipe the tear from my face.

"You're adorable, you know?"

"Am I?"

"Oh, for sure." I snort. "In another life I'm sure you'd be the girl of my dreams."

A tense silence settles in the air, and I'm overcome with the desire to punch myself at how pervy that statement came off.

"Hmm." She hums in a considerate tone while staring at me. "What are your dreams, actually?"

I sigh, relieved she didn't up and call me a lecherous weirdo before tucking and rolling onto the dirt road. "Um, yeah. I have dreams."

"What are they?"

"I'd talk about them, but they're more like nightmares. I don't like to dream."

"Gosh." she breathes. "I guess I understand. The spirits torture me all the time with their presence. Always barging in at the worst times and ruining my normal, you know?"

Boy did I, I thought, considering Kimmy's presence having the same effect on me. Whenever she was near, it felt like a haunting and obsession at the same time. My need to keep her close and away at constant war with each other, and Mikey, in my head.

"Do you have dreams?" I asked, gripping the wheel tight. "Like, aspirations, I mean."

She nodded, "Yeah, I do. I want to re-enroll into college and finish my Bachelor's degree in Exercise Science. It was once my dream to become a personal trainer and competitive swimmer, but I gave up on those a while ago..."

"Yeah? Since what?"

"Nothing."

"Um, okay." I uttered cautiously, afraid to upset her further than she already looked from the memory. I extend a hand to her, and grin at her curious expression. "Give me your hand."

She clasps my hand, and I note the trembling in her touch as well as the rush of heat that floods my core.

"Yes?" She chirps when I say nothing.

"Listen. I don't know all of what happened to you, or what made you drop out, but if you hear this from no one else on this farm, just know you've got a fan."

A lopsided smile crests her freckled face. "A fan?"

I nod. "Yup. I'll be your number one fan, cheering you from the sidelines and encouraging you to follow that dream if that's really what you want. Okay?"

She wipes her eyes with her free hand before nodding and pinning the sweetest look on me. "Thanks, Yvonne. No one's ever been my fan."

"Don't mention it," I say, just as I cruise by Zay's house. I glance out the window out of habit, to get a peek at the b-ball court where the guys and I met on the weekends.

I screech the truck to a stop when I see the sight, however.

"Whoa—what the—" Kimmy yelps at my sudden turn down the dirt road. "What's wrong?"

I don't answer as I surge on, my jaw flexing in anger at the sight.

Zay's house, the one he shares with his older sister Shay, can be seen from the distance as I pass by the dirt road before the town sign. Zay lived right before the main town could be seen, and the ramshackle house sat on a lonely acre of land on a slope. Peering into the distance, the basketball court could be seen as well as the four guys aptly battling for the ball. From where I'm sitting, I'm able to make out the tall four figures: Zay is faking with the ball in front of Malik, whose long arms swing and miss the opportunity to gain control of it. Bone rears up, and Zay passes him the ball where he ultimately dunks it with ease, as the tall half Latino guy is easily the tallest of them all at a staggering six-foot-six in height.

I jokingly anticipate Malik's furious roar at missing the pass and losing the game, but all humor stutters to the background at who I see slap him reassuringly on the back. The same asshole who violated my conversation, my space, and discussion with Mikey at the funeral. The one we were looking for but dreaded seeing again for fear of tearing his face off in the inevitable argument we'd fall into.

"Is that my brother over there?" Kimmy asks, mirroring the confusion in me. "Who are those guys he's with?"

"I know them." Is all I say before gearing the truck in reverse and cutting a left in the road towards Xavier Rose's house.

9

COUNT ON ME

"Look, it's Von!" Bone calls as I stomp towards the active b-ball game. I'm aware of Kimmy tiptoeing behind me by the suspicious looks the guys shoot us.

"Who's the bride?" Malik asks, referring to the white tea party dress I almost forgot she was wearing.

"Shut up." I bark, my eyes never leaving Zay's amused ones. "What's the meaning of this?"

He chuckles, dribbling the ball. "Of what? What did I do?"

"Oh, don't give me that, man. What is that bastard doing here balling on the court with you guys?" I jab an angry finger at Jeremy, who's gawking at us.

Zay retreats a step. "I don't know what the big deal is. The dude came over here and said he wanted to join in on the game. So, we let him in."

"Let him in?" I asked, narrowing my eyes suspiciously. "Just like that? He was such a jerk to me the other day. You were there for that. Why are y'all treating him like the best of pals or something?"

"Von," Bone cuts in, forever the mediator, raising his hands in defense. "Come on, chill out. You know it's not like that. We was just playing around."

"Yeah, that's all." Malik adds, and the crowd gathers around me like a tall flock of ravens circling their prey.

I glare at Zay again. "Sure, it is. What's the stakes?"

The guys go silent, averting guilty gazes in all kinds of directions instead of at me.

"Stakes?" Kimmy queries innocently. "What are y'all talking about?"

"Ask Zay," I grit out, my arms crossed as I single out my favorite homie and his actual gambling addiction. "What did you bet him?"

"None of your business, Von." Zay mumbles, turning around to throw the ball at the basket. It misses and falls back to earth.

I lurch for the ball, catching it before Zay could get a hold of it again.

"Zay!" I scream. "We talked about this, too. Remember what Shay said? You got to stop it with the gambling. She'll really kick you out if—"

I'm interrupted by a force knocking into me, so hard and abrupt it shoves me to the ground before I could make sense of it.

"Yo!" Zay snarls, and I look up to see the unthinkable.

"Nigga, are you crazy?!" Malik growls, and I finally get a grasp at what's just transpired. Jeremy was the force that shoved me to the ground, and all three guys gang around him— yelling shocked profanities and threatening to end him if he pulled something like that again.

Kimmy sinks to my side on the ground, her hands exploring my face for bruises.

"Hey!" She thundered. "Jeremy, what the fuck was that? Why did you push her like that?"

"Yeah," Zay growls at him, a threat in his tone. "Don't you ever touch her again, you hear me? I don't care how much money you offering."

"Money?" Kimmy fumes beside me. "Jeremy, what is he talking about?"

I somehow stagger to my feet, a little shaken, but otherwise unperturbed by the fall.

"Yvonne, honey, take it easy." Kimmy warns as she helps me to my feet.

"I'm all right." I tell her, my glare alternating between my favorite homie and the ginger asshole. Once I'm firmly rooted, I cross my arms as I regard them. "Let's play."

Just like the Tupac song, all eyes are on me after I bite the words out. Well, it's more of a challenge.

Jeremy's stormy green eyes find mine when he says, "You trying to play me?"

I nod once. "Yup."

He bursts into a maniacal laughter, the guys' glares trained on him. "You think I'm gonna play some chick? In basketball?"

He's the only one laughing, and I almost laugh too, because he truly must be new in town to not be privy to my reputation.

"I'll back you. Same as always." Malik volunteers, still glowering at Jeremy.

I shake my head at my other best friend and usual b-ball teammate. "Nah, it's all right. This'll be one-on-one. All or nothing."

Jeremy sobers. "One-on-one? The two of us?"

His eyes search the crowd as if to ask if I'm serious about playing this big bad boy sport all by myself. No one shares his disbelief, as he's only met with a collective crowd of trained hostility.

Bone looks as though he wants to kill him, while Zay's eyes are on me, wary and unsure.

"All right, y'all. Let's clear out. Give them some room to play." Zay says to us.

"Yvonne, are you sure?" Kimmy inquires softly, and it softens me a bit, but doesn't change my mind as I meet the concern in her eyes.

I nod. "Yes. I got this."

"I'll cheer you on from the sidelines, okay?" She whispers, filling my body with heat by using my previous offer of being her number one fan during our car chat.

"What are the stakes?" Jeremy asks once we're alone on the court. He's wearing that same smirk from the funeral that I want to punch off.

I dribble the ball, smooth and effectual, like his mocking tone doesn't even faze me. "If I win, then you call off whatever you bet with Zay. We'll pretend like it never happened, and you stay far away from me and my friends. Understand?"

Jeremy flexes his jaw, as if the idea peeves him, but otherwise nods. "Fine."

"Okay."

"And if I win," he adds, walking closer to me. "Then that deal between me and Zay is back on since I won that last game fair and square."

I clench my jaw, but nod. "Fine."

Jeremy glances between Kimmy and me. She's sitting on the sidelines next to Zay, who's biting his nails (an ugly habit of his whenever he's really anxious).

"As an added bonus," Jeremy states, an evil smile on his face. "stay off my family's property. And stay away from my sister."

Kimmy shoots to her feet. "Jeremy, no!"

"Deal." I agree, ignoring the pang in my chest at the thought of not seeing her again. Not seeing the scarred girl who was just like me.

"But..." Kimmy whimpers, and even though I'm not looking at her, I feel her pain radiating off her in waves, and Mikey stirs in my mind from it too.

"Vonnie, don't." He begs in my mind, but I shake my head as if to rid him from there.

I toss the ball—hard—into his bird chest.

"Game time." I grumble coldly, readying myself to win this game and shut this fucker up for good.

"Win this!" Mikey hisses, and I decide, like in my voiceless days, to let my actions speak louder than my words.

10

STORMY WEATHER

Three months fly by in a flurry of bad weather and heartache. I'm not being facetious when I say bad, either, since the news predicted some of the worst snow Richmond's experienced in over a decade.

The heartache, however? That came from Mikey. Since losing that basketball game and being forbidden to see Kimmy or even set foot on Aunt Stevie's property, he'd been the worst mind roommate to occupy a brain space with. While my chest ached at the thought of never seeing her again, my rational mind knew it was for the best I didn't see her. The ghost girl who did nothing but disrupt my stable, normal life. Disrupted my home and heart that skidded rapidly at the sound of her voice. Jeremy had been surprisingly adept at the sport, and even though my five-year winning streak against the guys was notable around these parts, it apparently did little in comparison to the basketball elite teen who played religiously in his former life in New Jersey, apparently. Maybe had I known that tidbit of knowledge then I wouldn't have bet so big, wouldn't have gambled my favorite homie's debt into a double down, all-or-nothing deal and lost Kimmy in the stakes.

No, I scolded, I didn't lose her. She was never "mine" to begin with. But I know in my heart that just didn't feel like the whole truth. Especially with Mikey's ill protests from the Mind Mansion.

"Kimmy wouldn't have made a bet so stupid, you know." He complained, much to my chagrin.

"Hush, bro," I say out loud, since I was the only occupant in the kitchen.

I squirmed with anticipatory delight, despite my sulking baby bro, in the creaky dining chair and being extra cautious in my movements so as not to glob any excess hair product on the tile floors. Since opening my heart to allow my adopted granny in and becoming an Honorary Carlson, we'd made my haircare a part of our Self Care Saturdays. We'd originally slated this luxury day to Sundays, but she and Aunt Stevie's titles as dual matriarchs of the farm community made that impossible. Sundays around here were like family reunions, existing as dinner parties or plain old cookouts with participants ranging from strangers, kids, to adults would bring a dish and do some electric sliding in the front yard. These communions took place at Aunt Stevie's or Mamma Dean's, and it was always so comical to observe the old ladies fuss about the weekly party's location.

So, Saturdays were best for our just-girls day. While my hair had always been a point of contention in my old life, the one I loathed, since all it had been used for was a pulling weapon, an item either Lucy or her boyfriends would yank to force me into submission or silence. Mamma Dean always insisted I take care of it, saying I was, "doubly blessed from the best to have tresses so good," and that if I wouldn't maintain my waist length hair, then she would. So, fast forward to the present, and here this day was born, from my loving, often pestering, Mamma Dean.

"You feel that pre-poo on your scalp, yet?" She asked, hobbling into the kitchen rocking her ruby red bathrobe.

I blink, forcing myself back to the present. "Oh, yeah! It's super moisturizing. Feel it all the way to my bones."

She shot me a droll look as she occupied the chair next to me. "Vonnie the clown, I should call you. Always got jokes."

I couldn't contain the chuckles rippling from my chest. "How's your hair, so far? You ready for me to wash it out?"

Mamma Dean dipped a tentative finger in her twin shampooed mane. "I think it's bout ready to be washed."

"I got you." I volunteer, standing up, but frown when she waves me away.

"No problem, child." She says. "Let me wash yours first."

"You sure?"

"Yes, ma'am." She insists, rising and guiding me to the large farmhouse sink. "Come on, now. Time to wash this out. This is *my* hair after all."

I smirk. "Don't you mean, *my* hair?"

"No. I meant what I said. Since I'm the one God called to take care of it. All that new growth is 'cause of me."

I search for the humor in her voice as I lean over the sink to prepare for the washing, but I sense none when the faucet runs.

"All them cuts and sores in your scalp when I started keeping up with your hair washing." She tuts angrily, and I'm sure she believes the rush of water deafens me, but my heart stutters at her next words. "People like Helen got no business raising chill'un. Never understood what my Eddie saw in that evil woman..."

I fight, and I mean hard, to stay in the present, but the combination of her fingers in my hair and derision in her statement jolts me into a dark room. In the mansion. Oh, fuck.

Suddenly it's dark, and I have to blink several times to get the gist of my whereabouts. A white door materializes and I'm crumpled into a ball as I listen for the doorknob noises. Just one night, please, one night, I plead inwardly, at the thought of seeing her again. Of witnessing the woman I once referred to as "Mommy" with such trust and adoration turn that knob to my room when she was sure Devin was asleep down the hall. Because my big brother would never allow this, would never let us stay as a family together if he knew what really happened during the night.

Just give me one night of peace, I beg again, but my prayers go unanswered at the sound of the doorknob being jiggled open. No, no! I whine on the inside and turn to face the empty wall that was once lined with Mikey's T-Rex pictures.

"Hey, hey, pretty." A male's voice, I forget this one's name, croons in the dark.

I hold my breath, but don't respond. Maybe I should scream, the thought enters and leaves my mind as soon as it comes. I hug myself tighter in a frail attempt to ward off the inevitable.

And then there's her voice.

"Vonnie!" She hisses from the door frame. "Vonnie! You awake?"

Per usual, I say nothing, but allow my sniffles to serve as an answer to that ugly question.

"Vonnie, baby, Mommy needs another favor. You gonna help me out?"

A hand strokes my arm, and I jerk away, animal-like yelps escaping my mouth.

"Hey, calm down. It's only Mommy. It's me."

My lip trembles as I roll to the farthest side of the bed, away from her. "M-Mommy?"

I can't see her, or anything in this dark room my twin and I once shared, but I hear her smile. "Yes, baby. Mommy needs another favor, okay?"

Hot tears stream down my face as I shake my head at her, and though she can't see me either, she must sense my lack of consensus because she adds, "Vonnie, just one more time, okay? Vincent just wants to give you a little kiss. Mommy's sick, remember?"

I nod slowly, remaining silent.

Oh, she's gotten used to this game of night talking, because she continues.

"I'm sick, okay? And, uh, Mr. Vincent got the medi-cine I need to get better. But I won't get better if I don't pay him first. That's how you can help me. Just do me this one favor, and this'll be the last time. You have my word."

I open my mouth to scream, to yell out for my big brother's rescue, but I...I can't. The sound is literally trapped in my throat, and only sobs make their way through.

"N-Nnnooo..." My broken plea comes out more like a terrified moo, and I'm trembling so hard I feel my brain rattling in my skull. That's what she always said after she asked for one of her "favors," and still the torture came, nightly, to my room. The favors didn't happen that much when daddy and Mikey were still around, but since moving back from New York and Uncle Troy's house, she got sloppier, bringing guys into my room whenever Devin left the house whether it be day or night.

"Vonnie, with the pretty pretty hair." The man's voice came again, making me cringe further into myself. He got closer, I realized, since the stench of liquor grew stronger all of a sudden.

"N-N—" I mumbled, but the calloused finger found my lips and traced them.

"Shh, girl." He garbled as soon as the zipping noises penetrated the night air. "You don't want no harm to

come to your sick mama, right, Vonnie with the pretty
pretty hair?"

A hand tugs at my afro, and all of a sudden, I find my
voice.

"No!" I scream, praying for this newfound
sound to be my salvation from this man. From
this place.

"Vonnie! Vonnie!" Mamma Dean shouts, before
dropping her voice down to a gentle whisper.
"Baby, calm down, it's alright."

My eyes work overtime to gather my sur-
roundings again. Mamma Dean is cradling me
to her body as I take in the sight of the rus-
tic kitchen. There's no white door. No man with
his liquor-laced breath and menace in his touch.
There's no Mommy, either, but I'm not sure if I
ever had her.

"Shh," she croons, and I know she's crying because her next words are sort of broken, "please,
stop shaking, baby you scarin me! I'm sorry, I'm
sorry!"

"W-What...?" I try to ask her why she is so sorry,
for what she was apologizing, when she continues.

"I didn't mean to bad mouth your mama, it's all
my fault. It scares me when you have these fits.
Come on, let's sit you down, now..."

I'm escorted to a chair, and my arms are shaking as I wrap them around myself.

She rubs my back firmly, hovering before me and studying my distant eyes. "Get yourself together, Vonnie, come on. You got this, baby. Put the blame on me this time."

I stare at her, finally seeing her, and the tears she's forced to speak through though I know she's hurting like I am.

I hugged her. "Where am I?

"Home," she sobs, returning the hug and anchoring my body and soul to this realm. "You home. You're back."

I nod, not fully believing her for a reason foreign to me, and try to stand on shaky legs.

"Ease up, now girl." She urges as she helps me up. We're hobbling down the hall, and my hair is sopping wet and trailing a path I know she's going to fuss me out about. However, the reprimand never comes, even as she escorts me to the large master bedroom in the back of the house. It's her room.

"Your legs don't look fit to climb them stairs right now. Take a rest in my room, all right?"

"But—"

"Don't fight me, girl. Just go on and lay down and I'll bring you some leftover gumbo Petina made yesterday."

"Okay." I allow her to towel dry my tight curls before laying me down and tucking me in. My stomach roils, however, at the thought of eating the soup Petina Alvarez, our Hispanic neighbor and Bone's mother, prepared for the cookout yesterday.

"I'll pass on the soup, if that's all right?" I whine, the room still slightly spinning.

She opened her mouth to protest, then held her hands up in defeat. "Yes ma'am. I won't bother you again unless you call me, okay? I'll be in the kitchen, cleaning up our pre-poo disaster."

I half-smiled, feeling rather ashamed at yet another time slip ruining things for me.

She placed the gentlest of kisses on my forehead before leaving. The last thing I heard before falling back into a fitful sleep was my phone chirping.

II

I HAVE TO GO

"Vonnie, I really miss her. Can we just check and make sure she's okay?" Mikey asks emphatically as my eyes drift open.

Not a dream, I think as I study the now pitch-black room. Not my room. The blackout comes back to me as does the guilt at ruining our just-girls day, but my head is spinning too much to stop and feel too bad about it.

"You already know the answer to that," I mutter as I attempt to rise from the bed. Uneasiness filled me as I sought to navigate the darkened room that was not my own. Where was Mamma Dean? She'd made it a habit to go to bed a little after six in the evening, and judging by the ominous darkness outside I'd guessed it was way later than that.

"Vonnie," Mikey asserts, *"are you all right? You really gave Mamma Dean a scare earlier when you had those thoughts about Mom."*

Anger boiled my blood at his choice of words, making me stumble back onto the bed from its intensity.

"I'm just fine. And that woman is no mother of mine." I growled.

His answer was instant. *"We've talked about this. Just because she was shitty, doesn't make her any less our mother. You know what you need to do."*

"What's that?"

"Forgive her."

"Over my cold, dead body in the ground." I catch myself retorting. Maybe farm life was sticking to me, as I recognized that borrowed phrase of Cousin Dan's.

Mikey sighs. *"You have a bad habit of holding on to things. Both of us do, I know."*

I frowned at that. "Huh? No, I don't. I just have my convictions. And one of them is hating her. Don't you remember what the doctor said? Don't you get it? She took both of our futures away."

I squeeze my eyes shut as the memories of that excruciating pain in my pelvis returns. After one of her "favors," I began to experience intense menstrual cramps. Only, the pain intensified after a full week of popping pills and suffering, since I had a fear of doctors and wanted to wait until I knew for sure it was life or death pain. When I woke up on the fifth day of suffering, I collapsed and woke up in Mercy Hospital. Most was a blur after that...as if the memories existed on old school videotape. I don't recall the name of the disease, but whatever it was, ate holes through my cervix and was the root of all that pain the doctor's deemed only emergency surgery could fix.

I wrapped arms around my suddenly chilly body, shivering from the images and utter emptiness. "I can't let go. She's the enemy."

"She's dead." Mikey continued softly. *"But you're not. You're still here, and have the chance to forgive her. To let it go and be better—"*

"Shut up, Mikey!" I roared in agony. "Stop playing therapist. Just...stop!"

"Okay, okay." he hedged. *"Then why take it out on Kimmy? If hating Mom isn't holding you back, then what is?"*

"I..." I begin futilely, unable to find the right counter argument. "I'm not..."

"Can you honestly say that you're not projecting? That you don't resent her because she's just like you?"

I released a huge breath I don't notice I'm holding as the truth of his argument pierces the hurt in my chest. It pierces it more sharply than the agonizing memories do, and I struggle to find a reason to disagree, but...

I stand to my feet, my resolve still shaken, but adrenaline filled in the gaps as I headed to the bedroom door.

"Where are we going?"

I clear my throat, terror and indecision splitting me almost in two. "Going to see her."

"Kimmy?" Mikey exclaims, his joy so infectious it melts the ice around my heart a little. *"Really? Right now?"*

"Yup."

"But what about the snowstorm?" He queries, and I smile.

"I'll take my coat."

A beat, then he counters, *"But what about Jeremy? You lost that bet and he forbade you from the property."*

I never got the chance to question Zay about the ramifications of that bet, but I'm damn sure he wouldn't give me details anyway since he barely responded to my texts these days.

I'm pulling my winter parka over my t-shirt and pajama bottoms as I respond to Mikey.

"He forbade me from his sister, too, and yet here we are. Sneaking over there right now to go and see her, *Killer Silence* style."

"Espionage!" Mikey quips excitedly, referring to the spy game we both loved. *"Vonnie on that G shit!"*

I giggle agreeably as I study my suited self in the full-length living room mirror. It was now or never, I coached myself, feeling that familiar fear of reality rise up again.

"What's your plan?" Mikey asks.

"Making it up as I go along, bro." I respond, before trudging to the front door.

Peering through the sliver of door window I notice the beast: The snow is so ferocious it illuminates the dark front yard from the thick blankets on the ground. I'm not quite sure I'd ever seen snow this harsh, not even in colder DC, but I steel myself anyway to face it. To face the fight of what was to come and try kindness with her. Mikey was right; I saw so much of myself in her tortured green eyes, and felt like the only one who resonated with how haunted by past ghosts she was. We were one in the same, and…well, she was interesting to look at. I wouldn't deny that. I couldn't deny the pitter patter of my heart noises whenever we connected eyes, or the urge to just hold her, to shield her from the horrors of demons that taunted her on a daily basis. I'm testing my distaste of Mikey's love for her, and find none as the heat fills my cheeks and rushes to my center. Fuck it, I thought, the need to just be near her outweighed both Jeremy's and the snow storm's threat of danger in that moment.

But a smell stops me dead in my tracks.

I recognized that punch of cherries and lavender, and before I could react, a pair of arms seized around my middle just as a scream erupts from my throat.

12

STRONGER THAN YOUR LIES

I twist and thrash violently to escape the intruder's arms. Their arms are surprisingly weak, as it took little effort to break out and face the bastard.

More like, the bitch.

The one from my past, at that, whom I tried in earnest to avoid.

I blinked hard, as I struggled to make sense of this. Was this reality? A timeslip? How on earth was *she* here?

"Sylvia?" I hiss, and while there is little light in the living room, I can easily make out her form.

Her thick black coat swallows her middle, making it difficult to glimpse at the changes life and hormones wrought on her body. Her honey blond hair is longer and falls in thick rivulets down her back. The last time I saw Sylvia Blake was in that other life, right before leaving for

Virginia when her family fostered Devin and I for a few months.

"I told you; you couldn't keep hiding from me, Vonnie Masters." She smirked, tossing a blond lock over her coated shoulder.

I'm still astonished when I ask, "How the hell are you here right now? Is this...is this real?"

She nods, smiling. "Yep. Sure is. If you'd responded to my text messages, you'd see that I told you I was visiting. I got a job teaching at Macon Middle school."

"Macon Middle?" I ask, my voice distant as I try to piece together meaning. I almost kicked myself for ignoring that text I received before falling asleep. "As in, the local junior high school in town?"

She only nods as another huge smile spreads across her face. "I told you I'd come and visit when I could. Well, now I'm here full time! Isn't that great? Dad was thrilled when I told him about the teaching gig and that you lived here."

"Right..." I whispered, and I couldn't resist adding, "Or do you mean he's thrilled that Devin lives here?"

A tic works its way in her jaw. "Does it matter?"

"Wow." I blew out.

"That sweet old lady let me in when I got here an hour ago." She continues as if there's no wrong in that statement. No lies or deception that's always threatened us. "She left and said not to disturb you since you had a rough day and needed the rest. So, I waited for you out here. And here we are."

Like usual, she provides all the necessary answers to my unspoken questions. For all intents and purposes, she was perfect. Groomed since birth to be the gorgeous and righteous preacher's kid, totally destined to become the perfect wife to a perfect groom.

"Carlson." I mumble absently, my legs weakening as I listened on.

"What?"

"Carlson. That's my name. I don't go by Vonnie Masters anymore since—"

To my further shock, she slaps me so hard I see spangled stars when I recenter.

"The fuck was that for?" I demand as I cup my affected cheek.

Her pale face glowed bright red in anger as she yelled, "What do you mean that's not your name? You got married?"

I rear back, and cup my face in my hands. She was draining the little energy I had left after that

timeslip. I open my mouth to answer her outrageous claim, when a knock comes at the front
door behind me.

We both freeze.

"Expecting company?" Perfect Sylvia questions,
and I note the latent panic in her voice.

I shake my head and turn around in my original
path to open the front door. Just what the hell
was this day? I wondered, bewildered by the confrontation of so much past for one day I found
my eyelids getting heavy again. I'll answer the
door, send Sylvia away, then get some more rest.
Yes, a good plan, I determine. Besides, if it wasn't
Mamma Dean, then it was probably Cousin Dan
or another neighbor or church member stopping
by to check on her. I'm excited to send them away
and get the interaction over with when I twist the
knob.

"You're awake!" Mamma Dean blurts as she
rushes inside. "Back to the world of the living.
Why you all dressed up? Y'all eat yet?"

"I..." I'm stuttering to answer her onslaught of
questions, but not from the biting winds that rush
inside the open front door.

Mamma Dean continues talking, not seeming
to notice me frozen at the front door still. "They
lost power in the storm and need to stay a few

nights here. You go ahead and make them, and your little friend there, welcome while I start cooking."

Oh, no. The nervous stammers come from the triple set of green eyes that bore into mine.

"Can we come in?" the lady I recognize from Aunt Stevie's funeral, who everyone calls Viv, stammers.

"S-Sure!" I leap out of dodge to allow a shivering Viv, Jeremy, and Kimmy inside the warm farmhouse.

Viv enters the house robot-style from the cold, and she's wearing a huge red fur coat and leggings that accentuate her round bottom, but also appear too thin to offer any protection from the blizzard outside.

Jeremy stomps past me without giving me a second thought as he disappears into the kitchen, and Kimmy creeps inside timidly, as if there's a bomb set to detonate at her arrival.

The three of us, Sylvia, Kimmy, and me pass awkward stares between each other in the living room entrance. My mouth is suddenly Sahara dry, and I work to moisten it to get some words through.

"I'm Sylvia," Sylvia offers, extending her hand to Kimmy.

Kimmy shakes it, her eyes still watching me as if I'd strike her at any moment. I hate the fear in her eyes, that I was the reason it was there.

"Nice to meet you." She tells Miss Perfect.

Sylvia crosses her arms across her chest, studying Kimmy suspiciously from head to toe. "What's your relationship with Vonnie?"

"Relationship?" Kimmy gasps, retreating back a step until her back hits the door. "It's not, I'm not, we're not—"

"Good." Sylvia cuts in, wrapping her hand around the back of my neck to bring our lips together. Her kiss is quick, but persistent, and before I can rip my mouth away, she pulls back to toss Kimmy a smug smile. "For a second, I thought you were crushing on my girlfriend."

Everything pauses.

There she was, standing right within reach when I steeled myself to brave the storm to see her. To hold and encourage her to come out of her shell with me. I had so much to tell her, as did Mikey, but all that comes out as I gawk at her frightened face is a broken, "Sorry," before I turn on my heel and bolt upstairs, away from the demons that waited for me in reality.

13

SUGAR

I make it to the sanctuary of my bedroom and rush to lock the door behind me. I wait an extra minute leaning against the door for my breathing to steady, but there's only more pounding in my ears as I do. The room spins momentarily as I limp to the bed in the center of it, frantically attempting to gather my thoughts on what just happened.

Sylvia Blake, my girlfriend, was here.

I don't quite recall when I picked up the PlayStation controller, but I find myself as Svetlana, the badass catsuit-wearing corporate spy in *Killer Silence 2*, my cherished video game.

My mind drifts to the story of our relationship as I'm playing, and the immediate shame and hurt that follows. We met when I turned twelve years old, and she was fifteen, and at first we developed a kind of sibling bond, since I never had a sister. She was refreshing to hang out with, and it only made sense that our relationship would strengthen after moving into the Blake household. It didn't. After overhearing her and Brenda, her visiting cousin, discuss her true feelings for me, that I was the first girl she'd ever loved, it felt like I was floating on cloud nine in elation. Somebody loves me, I thought, giddy from delight after what I eavesdropped. I'd almost started dancing outside her bedroom door, when her next admission froze me in place.

"Uncle Tim ain't gonna like the idea of you liking girls," Brenda said in response to Sylvia's confession to loving me.

Sylvia sighs. "I know. It's not right, or godly, but I have feelings for her, B. What am I supposed to do, huh?"

Brenda made somewhat of a gagging noise before saying, "Ugh, true. Can't say I'm thrilled about it, either. You got to come clean and tell your parents."

"What? No! Daddy will freak out!"

"You're missing the point! Don't you see it? You're not gay, Yvonne and her brother are just agents of the devil. They're the sinners, and they're what's wrong with you. They have to go."

"I'm already lying to them. I told my parents I want to date Devin, and they loved the idea, but it isn't true. I love her, but I can't keep lying to my parents to be with Yvonne."

"End the charade then. They have to go." Brenda reiterates coldly. "Are you trying to go to Hell?"

A pause, then Sylvia whispers. "I...I can't do that to them. They've been through so much. I mean, they practically have nothing. No family. No friends. No home..."

"Well," Brenda snapped. "If you don't do something about this, then I will. I think I know just what to do."

"What's your plan?"

I don't wait to hear Brenda's hastily concocted plan to abort us from the Blake household. The steel ice around my heart strengthened that day, and I wanted nothing but revenge from then on against the girl I gave my heart to. I'd planned on finding a guy, any guy really, from Pastor Tim's church to seduce. I hadn't really meant to sleep with him, just needed to make out with the patsy then allow myself to get caught by Sylvia. My heart soared at the prospect of hurting her the way she hurt me. The plan was simple, clear cut, except, everything went wrong. Instead of Sylvia, it was Devin who discovered us together, and when I tried explaining reason to him, his eyes got this far away look before he passed out.

I thank God, every day, Devin and I got out of that house when we did. The timing of Mamma Dean connecting with us had been suspiciously perfect, considering our stay with the Blake's would definitely end after all that happened with the patsy I used from their church and Brenda's accusation of Devin "manhandling" her in his bed. She didn't outright say it was "rape," but the threat was clear: they wanted us out. The sinful kids. The hellions who brought dysfunction wherever they rested their heads.

To my surprise, the hours fly by without disturbance from anyone, not even Mamma Dean calling to say the food was ready. It was around midnight, and my eyes throbbed from the strain of staring at the twenty-four-inch flat screen in my room. I stand up from the beanbag chair to stretch when the sharp pain hits my bladder. The urge to pee is so insistent I all but fly to the bathroom down the hall. I almost burst inside, like usual, since no one else really used this bathroom except me, but stopped when I heard someone growl, "I already paid you half of what we agreed on, man. Don't pussy out on me now!"

The gruff Jersey accent belonged to no other, I thought, than the ginger asshole. Jeremy.

"I'll tell her everything. Remember our bet. Do this, or everything comes out."

He pauses to allow the other person on the phone to respond, but not long before he snaps again. "Just do it. If I have to see that bastard one more time, I'll do it myself. But you know what that means if I do. Fucking Shame!"

A knot forms at the pit of my stomach at the prospect of who he's talking to, more like threatening, and the old anger from the game rises before I can refrain myself.

"Out!" I bark, relishing in the frightened yelp he emits while turning to face me.

"Oh. It's you." His tone is dry as he assesses my pajama clothed body. "You hear any of that?"

"And if I did?" I challenged, crossing my arms.

He tousled his red curls. "I don't have an answer for that, to be honest."

I stalked close to him. "I don't know what you two were discussing, but that better not have been Zay. Because if I hear that you were threatening my friend, I'll be sure you live to regret it. You're the fucking shame around here. Not him."

Power radiates through me as I spit his bitter retort back at him.

However, the nervous edge disappears as he listens, and a crooked smirk forms on his face. "Right. *I'm* the Shame."

"Damn right." I reinforce the words with blatant menace, daring him to challenge me.

"Okay." he laughs, and it feels almost as if I'm the butt of the joke when says, "You have a nice night, Rude Girl."

He makes it to the hallway in that confident saunter of his when I scream, "You ginger asshole!"

He guffaws as he disappears around the corner, to the guest bedroom farthest from mine.

Just what the hell was so funny? I ponder after I finish answering nature's call. And just what the hell were the stakes on that bet? Was Zay in danger? There were so many questions needing answers, I kind of lose my train of thought and direction as I wander down the hall. Except, I don't stop at my bedroom door, but keep walking. I walk until...well, I don't know how I intuit where she'd be, but yank my hand away from the nearly turned knob when I notice my actions.

"*Go in.*" Mikey encourages softly. "*Just walk in.*"

"What?" I hiss, sort of dazed that I'd just wandered in front of this guest bedroom.

"*She's in there, you know.*"

"I...I don't think she'll want to see me." My voice is small as I consider them, and believe them to be true. After knowing her feelings for Mikey, it felt just wrong to flaunt Sylvia in her face like that. In fact, I'm sure of a feeling before I answer my mind-mansion brother. "I hurt her."

"Yeah, you did. But she loves us. She'll understand if you explain it to her. Trust her."

Trust her. Trust her. To do that, I noted, I needed to trust myself to be real. After spending so much time in my mind and in the past, I never considered firmly rooting myself to the ground. Not for me. Not for anyone, but in that moment I want to. I want to be there for her, and talk to her.

Do this, Vonnie, I coach myself inwardly as my hand finds the golden knob to Kimmy's room.

Now or never.

The knob twists, but not from my hand, and I soon find myself gawking dumbly at the girl at the threshold.

14

DINING ROOM

"K-Kimmy?" I sputter.

"Oh, Yvonne." Kimmy mutters, a glint of hope lit in her eyes, but only for a moment before sadness replaced it. "It's you."

"This was a mistake. I'll get out of your hair."

"No, wait!" She titters frantically, grabbing my arm. "I'm sorry. Feel like I'm always ruining things for you."

I frown as I regard her hand on my arm. "Babydoll, no. How can you think that you're the problem? It's me. I know you love Mikey, and I shouldn't have flaunted Sylvia in your face like that."

Her eyes saucer as she listens, her hands falling at her sides. "Mikey?"

"Um, yeah. You two love each other, right?"

Her green eyes jet from left to right, surveying the hall before hissing. "Come in."

"Kimmy, wait—" She pulls me into the room after my small protests, and my heart races at the sound of the door closing behind me.

"Come, sit with me. Okay?" She's still speaking and ushering me towards the queen-sized bed in the corner. The room, like the rest of the guest bedrooms in the farmhouse mansion, is neatly decorated with a bed and a lone chest of drawers in the corner. The decor puts me in mind of southern debonair, with frilly white lace curtains and old-timey bedding.

Kimmy ushers me to the bed, where we sit and face each other fully. There's a determination in her eyes I have never seen before.

She takes a huge breath. "Whoa. That was huge for me."

"Yanking me into your room?"

"Well, yeah. I told you; physical contact is really not my thing. In fact, it sort of scares me to feel someone else's skin on mine."

I almost called that bullshit, considering what she'd done with Mikey at the lake, but her hands were trembling insanely. They shook so bad I almost reached out, but remembered that touching her would worsen her fear instead of soothing her. I settled for resting my hands on my thighs.

"I want to know more about you." I say, heart thumping and thudding in fear of her response. Fear of being thrown out.

Her eyes widened. "Really?"

"Yeah."

"Why? I thought you wanted nothing to do with me after that bet with Jeremy..."

"About that." I held up my hand to interject. "That was my bad. I shouldn't have bet you over anything. You're a person, a woman, with feelings and her own mind. Sorry."

"What are you really doing here, Yvonne?"

"I...I want to get to know you. Honestly. I really think you're interesting because you're so much like me. I know I'm not the only one who feels it. This insane connection between us."

"You aren't. I really like you."

"Then that tears it." I extended my hand to her. "Vonnie Carlson, nice to meet you darlin."

"Kimmy Gresham. Nice to meet you too. This is nice."

A long bout of silence stretches and distorts the air between us, the tension heightening after every passing second.

"Why were you dressed like that when I came to your house that day?" I asked, the silence driving me crazy.

She blushed, hugging herself. "What do you mean? Dressed like what?"

"You called me Jenna and your eyes turned white..."

She sighed. "That sounds like something I'd do."

"What I mean is what's the deal with that ghost shit?"

She chewed her lip nervously before answering. "I told you. I see spirits."

"Kimmy, I just want to get to know you. That's all, and I understand that I pretty much fucked up the right to ask anything of you after I wagered you in that b-ball bet. So, if you want to tell me to fuck off, you can. I'll leave right now if that's what you need."

Her voice was so soft, so low, I barely heard it.

"Jenna was my niece, my older sister's daughter."

"So, you have an older sister?" I asked.

"Yeah. She's in prison back in Jersey."

"You mentioned your niece in the past tense. Jenna's no longer around?"

A weak smile crests her face. "She was killed."

"Did your sister—"

"God, no!" She snarled defensively. "She'd never hurt anyone. Liz is the kindest person I know. My best friend. The only one who believes in my ability to see spirits. Jenna would've been five today. So, whenever her spirit visits I try to make her feel welcome. She loves to play Tea Party, so...that's what we do."

I thought about my relationship with Devin. I once thought he hung the moon. Her fierce devotion to her older sister is something I recognize and respect. Even though he left me behind to enlist, feeding into all of my abandonment issues, I still loved him. Still thought that, even though he was human, he still had the supernatural ability to fly up into the clouds and hang the moon in the sky like always.

Kimmy shifts in her seat, as if uncomfortable. "I don't want to talk about this anymore."

"Cool with me." I agreed cautiously. "But I'm sorry to hear about your sister. I can tell she's a great person to be loved by you."

Kimmy's eyes pierced into mine, and for the first time, I'm not squirming under her gaze. I'm not uncomfortable. To my surprise, the urge to run away from the affection in her stare doesn't make me want to run for the hills. No. That lingering desire to hold her...flares up and strengthens with an intensity like no other.

Taking a breath for courage, I reach out for her. "Can we just lay here?"

Her green eyes are eying me like a CT scan. "Is this...is this Michael?"

"Mikey." I correct evenly. "And no. This is me. All me. I want to be close to you. Please?"

"I..." Her voice trembles with indecision as she stares at my outstretched hand. "I don't know."

"I know you prefer Mikey. Trust me—he loves you too. But can we just be together tonight? You and me. Just Vonnie and Kimmy."

"And Sylvia?" She chirped.

The familiar guilt rears its ugly head at the mention of my ex and that terrible confrontation in the living room.

"She's nothing to me. Trust me. We had discussions a few weeks ago about possibly getting back together. But that's all it ever was. Discussion."

Her eyes slide around the room in consideration. "I believe you."

I release the breath I'd been unaware of holding. "Thank you!"

Her eyes fluttered shut and I watched her ease her back against the bed. When she's fully vertical, she reached her hand down, offering it to me. "Lay with me?"

My heart soars at her invitation, at her willingness to break her code of no-touching to honor my request.

I grab her hand, which quavers violently at my touch, and by the time I lay beside her, I find myself raising the shaky appendage to my lips.

"It's all right." I whispered silkily in her ear. "I will never hurt you."

"Okay." She chokes out, eyes shut and blushing.

"Look at me, Babydoll." Her eyes peel open hesitantly. "I see you." I say, placing another kiss on her hand. "I see you." I repeat, kissing her inner arm. "I see you." I'm trailing slow kisses up her arms until I hover before her lips. Our heavy breaths match as our eyes seek inside each other's souls.

"Vonnie!" Kimmy whines, her tone thick with need.

"Babydoll?"

Her small breasts heave in rapid up and down motions as she licks her lips. Her arms wrap around my thicker frame and she pulls me in close. "I want you. I see you, too. It's you I want. What I...what I need."

"Oh, Kimmy..." I breathe, before my lips meet hers. Our bodies fuse together in hard rubbing motions and I reach a searching hand below to cup her moist center.

"Vonnie!" She purrs, her body thrashing before me.

My body hums with a vibrating intensity and mouth waters at the prospect of tasting her like I always wanted to. Time and reality blends together as we taste, touch, and savor, not fear, the feel of each other.

"Somebody wants to talk to you." Kimmy's voice cuts through the dark room we fell asleep in.

"What?"

A lamp light turns on, and I now see her face is bright red with...embarrassment? In fact, I'm not sure what's happening anymore as she stares me down.

"S-Sorry." She stutters, sitting up and toying nervously with a strawberry blond curl. "I know this is all of a sudden, but he just won't leave me alone. He's been...following me since my grandma's funeral. Insisting I deliver a message to you."

My sleepy mind swirls from her crazy talk, and a pit forms in my stomach again, but this time from fear of the identity of this person stalking her.

"Who's been stalking you? Tell me if this is just ghost mumbo jumbo or if there's somebody after you. I can get you help."

She shakes her head. "No! I'm fine. Just please stop looking at me like that."

"Like what?"

"Like...that!"

My gaze slides around the room, and I feel awkward when I ask. "Like what?"

"Like I'm crazy!" She snarls, standing up to pace the floor. "That's how my brother looks at me when I tell him a spirit's visited. That's how Mom looks, too. She keeps saying I need meds. I don't! I just...they won't leave me alone. And you have no clue how it feels to be haunted by these spirits all the time and having no one believe you when you decide to open up. It's...it's—"

"Lonely." I finish for her, that familiar resonation rearing back up. I reach out to take her hand. "Kimmy, I'm sorry. I'm listening, okay? I'll hear you out."

She nodded, closing her eyes for composure. "Thanks. Didn't mean to spaz on you, but he's been visiting more often since I last saw you."

I nod, understanding, keeping my tone careful. "Okay. Can you tell me who it is? A spirit, right?"

A pause, then she whispers. "Do you know someone named Quincy? Quincy Masters, he introduces himself as."

I'm Black, and I never understood how Black people could go pale until she utters that name. All the blood drains from my face and I feel myself losing the battle for lucidity. One of those rooms…maybe it's a dining room…is beckoning me inside it within the Mind Mansion. I could easily slip away, fall into the dark room and not come out despite Mikey's protests. Maybe I should, I think, as I edge close to the forbidden door.

Hands grip my shoulders, shaking me. "Hey! Yvonne, stay with me. Come on!"

I blink hard, black splotches flash in front of my eyes and I can barely see her face.

"I see you, remember?" She croons softly, but urgently. "Find your center. It may help if you find the center of wherever you are, and focus on something."

"A…beacon?" My voice asks absently.

"Yes! Something like that. But right now, let my voice be that beacon. Don't slip away, sweetie. Stay here with me. Stay strong."

Suddenly, the floors and walls shrink away into thin air. The mansion, for the first time ever, dissipates at will as it nearly consumes me again.

"Kimmy?" My voice is hollow.

"Vonnie. I'm here." I'm in her arms, and she's holding me tight against her chest.

She spoke his name. The name of my first love, my father, who died under the most mysterious circumstances.

"You said...Quincy wants to tell me something?"

"Yes. He says he's your dad, but I'm scared he's lying and wants to hurt you. Some will do that. Lie to exact revenge on those they left in the living."

Her voice takes a hollow sound, as if she's lived through unspeakable truths of that nature.

"Quincy Masters is my father." I choke out around the emotion in my throat.

"Yvonne Carlson. Ain't that your name?"

"Now it is, yes, after Mamma Dean adopted me. I used to be Yvonne Masters in my other life."

"Other life." she murmurs, thoughtful as she turns to me in bed. "Did you want to talk to him? Or at least want to hear his message?"

Did I? I questioned myself. I wasn't so sure if the mere mention of him sent me flying into one of those dark mental rooms. But I had to be brave, like Mikey, and face this. Maybe she really was crazy, and maybe not, but I decided to indulge this insanity for the sake of my little brother's love for her.

For my love for her. The girl who was just as haunted as me.

Sighing, I nodded. "Let's do this."

"Okay." She agreed, closing her eyes. "H-He's here! I feel him all around us." After a long pause, she tilts her head to the left, as if listening to someone on the other end of a phone.

"He says...he's proud of you. That you've grown into a lovely young woman. He hates that he can't be there for your...wedding?"

"Wedding?" I gasp, fully expecting Kimmy's shocked green eyes on me, but to my surprise she keeps them shut. As if her only importance is accurately transcribing this ghostly message.

"It's a little unclear. Please, Quincy, slow down. I can't tell Vonnie until you calm down."

A moment, a slight sliver of a moment of hesitation slips by, making me want to turn tail and run back to stealing shit and taking names in *Killer Silence 2*, but Mikey's voice stops me.

"She's not lying." Mikey declared. *"It's him. It's dad."*

My eyes take in the room, as if searching for the tall dread-headed man that was our father, but all that greets me is a chill.

In fact, I'm shivering by the time Kimmy tilts her head to the right.

"Play the game, Vonnie." Kimmy orders in that same militant way Quincy used to.

I adjusted my position on the bed. "Excuse me?"

Kimmy's slender body lurches as if she wants to vomit, but only more sound comes out. "Game...play the game. Find Sommer. Talk to Sommer."

"Who is Sommer? Why do I need to talk to her?"

My heart drops to my toes, fear icing my veins as I observe my green-eyed girl convulse. I desperately want to reach out and hold her, to stop the shaking like she did with me, but I know I shouldn't, figuring this was the reason behind her "no-touch" rule.

"Vonnie," Kimmy calls in a strange monotone. "I'm sorry...piece of shit dad...I did not...abandon you. I'm here. Always here. Always...love you."

She seemed to be biting the words with waning energy, and I wanted to hear more, but my fear for Kimmy's wellbeing trumped all. Fuck this, I thought, fuck his message. I wouldn't put Kimmy's safety at risk to hear the apology he long owed me in his living years.

"Vonnie, wait." Mikey whispers. *"Ask him something for me, will you?"*

His direct request stunned me so bad; I froze. Mikey didn't usually ask me outright for things, insisting to rely on his ability to make me see reason to persuade me to do things at his will. So, this request I felt couldn't be ignored, no matter how scared I was for her.

"Okay." I replied.

"Ask him where he is. What it's like to be there."

"Wait, why do you want to know—"

"Just, please, Von." My brother implored brokenly. *"Ask."*

Taking a fresh gulp of cold wind, I do it.

Kimmy convulses again to answer. "Need to atone. Not home yet."

"How did you die, dad?" I blurt, knowing this will be all the information I'd care to know.

After Devin came home to our ramshackle New York apartment we occupied above a small grocery store in Harlem, he ran to our dad's room and threw items frantically into a tote bag. His eyes got a far away, horrified look, similar to the one he got when he found me with that patsy at the Blake's house. After ordering me to pack a light bag, we left for good the one-bedroom flat I knew as home since Mikey's death. Devin ignored all of my questions, but I remembered him mumbling every so often into a cell phone, something about wiring funds and moving to the final safehouse in Jersey. We traveled all night to Uncle Troy's, Lucy's older brother, house in suburbia, where he grumpily received us. I recalled the huge wads of cash Devin gave him, saying we'd "be no trouble, and out of your hair in a couple weeks." I never got what I needed, only some lame explanation from Uncle Troy that my daddy died. Lung cancer, he said. As did Devin. But I knew. Something awful happened and nobody let me in on it.

Another quiver, but an animalistic whine escaped her mouth when she answered, "Can't say."

I rose, out of fury, to jab a murderous finger her way. "Yes, you will. Just tell me! Why will nobody tell me what happened to you?"

A long pause beat by, and I'm convinced Kimmy's fell asleep, judging by all the wheezing she's doing. But I'm wrong. She rightens herself, opens her all-white eyes, and chants. "Devin's girl. Devin's girl. Burn Man...one bullet...tell her sorry for me."

"Devin's girl?" I demand. "Who's that? You're not making any sense goddamn it! And what the hell's a Burn Man?"

"She doesn't look so good, Von! Get her out of there!" Mikey hollers from inside.

His voice snaps me out of the anger for a second, and that's when I see it. The blood trickling from her eyes, nose, and ears as her body twists and thrashes out of control.

No-Touch Rule be damned, I lurched for her, gathering her shaking body in mine as I caressed her hair in the ice-cold room.

"Kimmy, baby. You there?"

More animal noises emit from her throat, but she doesn't stop shaking.

"Come on, now. Come back to me. Every time you're near me, I hear you. I see you from the mansion. I'm doing it for you now too. Just follow my voice. It's all right."

"Vonnie!" She screams, and the monotone disappears, leading me to believe Quincy has gone. "Help me! He...won't...let go. Get out of...me!"

"I don't know what to do!" I blubber in fear, holding her tight. Please God, I think, please help me right now. Whoever you are, wherever you are, somebody help her. I couldn't take it if I lost another person I loved to the darkness, to the madness unleashed from a hellion like me.

"Michael!" She howls, in that tone again, and I know it's him calling out to my baby brother. "Come. Come with me!"

"Leave us alone!" I spit, fuming at the man threatening the two people who lived inside my head and heart.

The room becomes a meat freezer, and I'm shivering alongside Kimmy as I shake my head in refusal. "Just go!"

"Vonnie," Mikey voiced. *"He's killing her. I don't know how, but...I see her life slipping away. Her soul is like, leaving her body or something. I won't let him take her! Go away!"*

"Yvonne!" A male's voice shouts from Kimmy's mouth. "Release him. Let him go home!"

"Fuck you!" I seethe, wanting so desperately to punch him, but resist due to the dying host body he's occupying. "Just go!"

"Keep my journal safe, Von. You hear me? I love her. I need to go get her. I'll be right back."

"What does that mean, Mikey?"

More silence as she continues to shake in my arms.

"Michael!" I wail, needing to reach him to understand what he means by those cryptic statements.

"*Shame*...all because of Shame. Shame, shame, shame!" Kimmy's chanting nonsense at this point, but I don't focus on it. I concentrate on my brother's fading presence slowly slipping from my mind. Leaving the mansion. Leaving me.

"I love you, sis." Mikey croons, his voice barely above a whisper. *"Keep Kimmy safe, and keep using that beautiful voice of yours."*

"No!" I choke out, and another minute passes. Another turbulent silent minute of the emptiness in my head. I don't feel him. It's so eerily silent and Kimmy is unconscious in my arms as I study her in the now-warm room. Tears prick my eyes as the urge to wither away overcomes me and the world blackens before I join the dead.

15

ATTIC

"You've got to go to her."

"...who are you?"

"It's me, darlin."

"You...I know you. I know that voice."

"It's all right. There's no time. Go to her."

"She doesn't need me. She's strong."

"Stop it, already! Both of you need to be there for each for what comes next."

"All I do is ruin her life. I'm better off here..."

"You're not. And you don't believe that."

"I don't know what to believe."

"Believe in her. Trust in yourself."

"Okay..."

"Listen, I can't stay too long. And you're in danger here if you linger."

"But I don't think I can keep on going."

"Stop it! Boss up and go to her. She needs you, and I don't think I can be there anymore."

"I'm scared!"

"I know. And it's okay to be scared. Some of the bravest people were scared first. Get out of here."

"Where is 'here?'"

"..."

"Hey! Where am I?"

"You're in the attic."

"In my granny's house?"

"No. I think she calls this place the Mind Mansion. It's where I used to live."

"This Mind Mansion was where you lived? Your home?"

"Yes. And no. I lived here, but it wasn't my home. Dad was right. It's my time."

"Where is home?"

"I'm still figuring that out...but we both have to find it. Leave this place and find home."

"Home..."

"Yes. And you know in your heart where that is. If you think real hard about it."

"I do...I do."

"Then tell me. Where is home?"

"It's...it's with her."

"Good to finally hear you admit it. It's almost time we switch places. Kimmy?"

"*Yes?*"

"*I'm really tired.*"

"*Me too, but...it's time I get going. To her.*"

"*Are you sure you're ready?*"

16

CAVING AND CRASHING

I grunted as the thick glob of syrup bursts through the flimsy plastic top to drench the previously dry pancake stack. A fit of rage rocketed through my being so powerful and intense I shot up from my seat and screamed my anguish before chucking the bottle across the dining room.

"Fuck!" I spat.

The entire room quieted and pinned nervous eyes on me. This anger was so...strange and new. Since waking up from that possession two weeks prior, it felt like I brought something back with me that didn't exist before. Like a new, bold, presence birthed from all that forlorn pain.

"Kimmy?" Viv, my mother, queried across from me. "Everything all right?"

I cleared my throat, eerily aware of my environment and company at that moment. "I'm all right. Just a little tired is all."

Mamma Dean adjusted herself in the brown wooden chair before chiming in from the far end of the rectangular table. "You just let me know if I can get you anything to drink, okay? I know these past two weeks have been especially hard on you since what happened to my granddaughter."

The light chatter that filled the room previously at Sunday brunch ceased and morphed into somber whispers. I hated this. I hated this so much I could spit fire and kill somebody, but at Mamma Dean's words I falter.

Sinking back into my chair, I run a shaky hand through my unkempt mane. I hadn't showered or washed my hair since Vonnie's incident.

Nothing really mattered to me anymore, and my days were often spent scavenging the fridge at nights for food, during times I knew the house would be otherwise vacant, before zombying back to Vonnie's room. To be beside her. To be there for her, like she was for me.

"Thanks, Mamma Dean." I mumble absently, forcing the tears at bay and failing.

"Sis, come on. You got to stop it with the out-bursts." Jeremy interjected. "You're twenty-two for heaven's sake, not twelve."

"Jeremy!" Mom scolds. "Leave her alone."

"Yeah," Sylvia, Vonnie's apparent 'girlfriend' who couldn't take a hint, or my blatant 'get the fuck out of here' warnings adds. "Maybe it's for the best if you get out of the house for a while. The snow cleared up last week and Richmond's been having some good weather. We can take a walk later on, if you'd like?"

Her gorgeous honey blond hair is pinned up into a neat bun and she's wearing a baby pink sweater and slacks. She looks like something off the set of *Grease,* with her Sandra D accessories and a demeanor sweeter than the pancake syrup I threw across the room. She's perfect and I hate her for it. I hate everyone these days, though.

"Everybody just shut the *fuck* up!" I roar at the chattering crowd consisting of Mamma Dean, Mom, Jeremy, and Sylvia's stunned expressions staring back at me as I stand.

"Kimmy, wait—"

I'm already running upstairs before Mom can finish her 'sweetie calm down' protest. She always does this, as a southern belle at heart she hates when I make a scene. Whenever I embarrass her.

Sylvia is right, after all. The snow did significantly melt away since when we got snowed in at Carlson Farms. To the untrained eye, it looks like a normal Spring day on the farm, and there really isn't much keeping me from going back home. Not home, I think, considering granny's house filled with bad spirits. Home was here. Where I was headed, just up the stairs, down the hall and to the right.

Vonnie's room.

I entered and forced the fake smile to arch my lips as I studied her. She looks so peaceful, in her bed and sleeping. She's been this way since we made contact with Quincy's spirit. When I woke up in her arms from the possession, I noticed her unconscious and barely clinging to life. Something was wrong. And it wasn't medical, despite the doctor's evaluation after the ambulance rushed her to the hospital in town. A coma, they called it. Said she experienced some sort of unexplained cerebral event that caused severe damage and that a medically induced coma would be the best hope in salvaging the healthy parts of her brain.

Two full weeks have gone by. And I never left her side. Though Mom and Jeremy went back home last week when the ice thinned out enough for travel, I insisted on staying here.

"Oh, let her stay." Mamma Dean insisted to Mom the morning she packed to leave. We were all standing in Vonnie's room, where her makeshift hospital room was, when the discussion of my leaving came up. "She won't be any trouble. Besides, she can help with Vonnie's daily care since they were such good friends and all. Right?"

"Right." I agreed, so thankful for the sweet old woman my granny insisted was her spiritual other half.

And now, here I was, patiently occupying the seat next to her bed, holding her hand and telling her about my day. I had no clue if this helped her, if she could even hear me, especially since I could no longer sense Michael's presence in her. But I had to try. I had to atone for bringing this evil spirit in her life that set out to hurt her. Thank fuck this Quincy was already dead, because I'd have killed him again if I were able to, for harming her. My Vonnie.

I massaged her hand, careful to avoid grazing the IV in her arm and ignore the tubes in her nose as I stared at her.

"Vonnie," I uttered with strained hope, "I'm really trying to get over this...this anger. It's all my fault you're in this condition."

Soft beeps echoed from the heart monitor in the air as my response. My heart...it was cracking. Splitting into several parts I wasn't sure all the hope and faux happiness in the world could bandage together. I pursed my lips in preparation for my daily ritual of calling on her brother, with hopes from somewhere in me that he'd respond.

"Mikey?" I breathed. No answer. Just like the other possible one hundred times I sought to beckon his previously forthcoming spirit.

"Please come back to me...both of you. I'm so sorry." My whimpers strangle me as I collapse into the chair.

"I told you she's dead. Dead as a doorknob." A familiar cold voice cuts into my agonized whimpers.

I flex my jaw in restraint before glaring up at my dead brother-in-law.

"Heath." I grumbled. "Go. The hell. Away."

His translucent body sort of floats to the opposite side of Vonnie's bed, bringing with it a cold chill in the air.

His dirty blond hair spills into his eyes, same as it did when he lived in the corporeal world, as he studied her face. "Listen, Kim. I know dead. And she's it. Your little friend here is gone."

My knuckles blanched at the pressure of my balled fists as I regarded him. "Did anybody ask your opinion? Are you a Shaman, or something? *You* barely know why you're existing in the In Between world either. So, what would you know about her being dead? Huh?!"

He shot me a 'duh' look. "Um, news to Kim. I'm dead. So, I know dead. She may not be there yet, but that little glow you living people got inside you? Well, I see that. Like now, yours is bright. But hers..."

"What? What do you see?" I hate the hope in my voice as I asked this dead jerk for any information about her welfare.

He cleared his throat. "Her light is there. It's really dim though. Might want to do something about that real soon."

"Do what?"

Heath got an awkward expression. "I said I know dead; didn't say I knew how to reverse it. That's all on you, kid."

Fury so hot surged through me I stalked toward the spirit that visited me almost daily since his suicide.

"All on me, huh?" I growl, my anger knowing no bounds at this point. "Just like Jenna's death is all on you? Didn't seem to be showing any sympathy to my sister when you killed her only daughter!"

A haunted look graces Heath Shay's see-through face before he flashes a sad smile at me. "Just like your sister Liz, you know just the right spot to hit. Right below the belt."

I almost deal with the sympathy manifesting at his sullen retort, but no. I don't back down from the tongue lashing he so desperately deserved. I jab an accusatory finger at him. "Don't you bring Liz into this! Jenna was her world, her everything, and you took advantage of your ex-wife in her lowest moment. You and that money-grubbing lawyer robbed her of everything! Now she's rotting in some prison for god knows how long and now you're no longer here for her to plead her case."

Heath sighs, giving me a droll stare. "Yeah, yeah. Well, I had my reasons. That druggie bitch tried to put me on child support after the divorce. I couldn't stand there and watch the empire I worked so hard to build from the ground up be destroyed. Drugged out vamp bitch is what she is, sucking me dry and leaving me for dead was her goal."

"I hate you." I sneered.

He shrugged. "Tough titties, Kim. You're all I got to talk to. So, I guess you're stuck with me."

I try to remember her words whenever I get this worked up, which is often, as of late. *I see you. Everything's okay. I see you. Everything's okay. Just find your center, Kimmy.*

The ramifications of that terrible ordeal, that awful court case that took the sweeter part of my family still haunted me. Mom fought hard to pay for Liz's legal team, even putting the house we were all raised in up for a second mortgage. As a single parent, Mom's Customer Service Rep earnings did little to keep the bills paid and I ended up dropping out of college to work nights at Lettie's Outlet, a local shoe store in East Orange, to help out with the failing mortgage payments.

But it was all in vain, since the judge threw my sister in jail for child negligence anyways. It was wrong, and I testified on my sister's behalf, but no one would hear it. Hear me. Mom always said that she'd rather die than return to Richmond to her mom's house. Said there were demons here she needed to stay buried, but those demons followed us constantly, it seemed. And here we were, me: a college dropout without any job prospects, Mom: withdrawn from everyone and batting away all of Mamma Dean's warm invitations to her Sunday communions, and Jeremy: a former basketball champ turned embittered loner. We were so broken. Broken spiritually and financially, and for this reason alone I suspected why Mom moved down to Virginia hellbent on bulldozing the house she was raised in.

Turns out, bulldozing a three thousand square foot farmhouse was much more expensive than she'd thought, causing her to put a pause on the demolition project and spend more fretful nights in it. Mom often got a fearful faraway look in her eyes whenever I questioned her about her childhood or the past. I loved my mom and hate that I can't help her with the ghosts that haunted her from when she was young.

I take a deep breath before calmly providing the jerk ghost with a response. "Heath. Please. Just go. I do not want to argue with you. I don't have the patience for your usual catty quips."

"Kim. Hey. I don't want to be alone. Why do you think I come here in the first place?" His voice still has its bored edge, but there's a latent desperation to it.

I rear back. "And I told you to stop visiting me! I need some peace and I won't do this in front of her. Don't you see she's resting?"

A smirk returns to his face. "She's *resting*, all right."

I'm now stalking the bastard. "She isn't dead! Nor is she dying! Just fucking go!"

"Auntie Kim?" A small voice utters between us. My heart drops as I stare into the ghostly chubby face of my would-be five-year-old niece.

"Jenna?" I ask in a voice equally as small as hers. "Sweetheart, what are you doing here right now?"

She tucks a stray blond curl behind her ear before mumbling, "I heard yelling. Are you mad at me?"

I dropped to my knees to caress her cold shoulders. "No, of course not! I'm, um, just a little upset."

"Upset?" She queries, as if toying with the word. "At daddy?"

"Um, well. A little." I reply, unwilling to lie to the little girl who's been the victim in all this.

Heath murdered her. Ended her life before ending his own, and violent things happened whenever the two souls occupied the same space. Like floorboards quaking or windows breaking.

I gulp, afraid of the inevitable shitstorm that's about to take place in Vonnie's room. Heath, previously composed and smirking judgmental eyes are now wide and as red as my hair. No, they're blood red as he observes the little girl between us. Jenna was the object of all his guilt and failures, and I normally took extra care to keep her inconspicuous whenever Heath invaded my space, but not today. I want to curse myself because I can usually sense Jenna's incoming presence, but I was so wrapped up in tearing Heath a new one that I must have ignored it.

A terrifying chill filled the room as I looked Jenna in her baby blue eyes. "Jenna, sweetheart. Time to play hide and seek, like from before, okay?"

Jenna's concerned frown hits me. "I don't want to be by myself, Auntie Kim. That dark house is big and spooky. Can I just sit with you like usual?"

"Failure!" Heath growled animalistically, his eyes now blood red. "No good! Failure!"

"Jenna!" I yelled. "Please go back to the house, okay? I'll drop by later to play Tea Party. Just, please run away from here!"

"No!" she whined defiantly, wrapping her arms around me like a vice. "Stay with you! Stay with you!"

"Jenna, please!" I begged, tears in my eyes as I witnessed Health's hollow body ripple like it usually did before objects were thrown across the room.

"Jenna!" Heath hollered, reaching for her.

"Aunt Kim!"

"Jenna, run!"

A slight tremor rocks the floorboards and I'm fighting to pry the dead girl's arms off. She isn't budging.

I rely on what I usually do when in the heat, or chill, of an angered spirit situation: I close my eyes and cast a silent prayer for the chaos to quiet. For the madness to go away, even for just a moment's peace.

Suddenly, everything stops, and the vice embrace of my timid niece disappears.

"Kimmy?" Mamma Dean's voice cuts through the mental fog.

I'm still kneeling when I notice her at the bedroom door. "Mamma Dean?"

Her purple tracksuit pants bunch as she further enters the room. "My goodness it's cold in here. Everything all right, child?"

Mamma Dean limped over to the chair beside Vonnie's bed and sat in it, expelling an exhausted breath. "This back of mine is killing me. Don't get old, Kimmy girl."

I almost smile at her wistful wisecrack, but I'm much too disoriented by her appearance as I stand up.

She cocks her head at me. "I'd ask who you were talking to in here, considering my granddaughter ain't quite up for much chit-chat right now, but I know you'll just feed me some lie about talking to yourself."

"Excuse me?"

She chuckles good naturedly, like there's a joke and I'm the unknowing punchline. "You know, after my Eddie died, I had nothing left in this world but pain, this big ole' house, and a ten-year-old son."

I watched her curiously, struggling to find meaning in her words. I argue with myself about throwing her out, but remember Vonnie was equally cherished by her as she was me. And that this was Mamma Dean' house. That she let me so kindly squat in to remain by my precious Vonnie's side.

Defeated, I slink to the chair beside her.

"That was almost fifty years ago." Mamma Dean breathes. "You know, when you lose someone you love so all of a sudden, it feels like the air itself will kill you by breathing. Like, a piece of your soul is ripped outta you, stomped, and chewed on. Point is, that pain feels impossible to peace out of."

I nod, my stomach twisting with a cold familiarity of that kind of loss. Losing my sister and niece within days of each other created an ache in my chest that never fully healed.

"I felt lost. I *was* lost. But then, a redheaded, firecracker of a girl introduced herself to me at church. We met and got along so well, and before I knew it, I made the best friend I'd ever had. Our kids became fast friends and we spent our holidays and weekends together. She was one of my favorite people. Had a spirit like the sun, it just drawed you in."

I straighten, staring at her. "You mean, my Grandma Stevie?"

She nodded, wearing a sad smile. "That's right. Your grandma and I met at an interesting time in our lives. Her marriage was a violent disaster and I was still grieving my late husband, and we formed a sisterhood of sorts to get each other through it. When Eddie junior asked about his daddy and began fighting at school, I sought comfort with her company. Same thing with your grandma Stephenie: there were nights her ole' man beat her so bad all she could do was drag herself back to bed and call me. I'd rush over there and be by her side. Just like she did for me."

I'm reminded of the turbulent spirits that occupy that huge house of my granny's. And the one that especially made my blood run cold whenever I entered it for a reason that had nothing to do with the weather.

I gulped before whispering, "Seymour."

She nodded again, staring out the window. "Yep. That's your grandpa. A mean sport. He loved that bottle more than he ever did Stevie. I did my best to keep her here in this world. Tried my hardest to keep those demons off her even when Viv ran away. We had so much in common, Stevie and me, that it seemed like our tragedies kept lining up. After Viv gave birth to your brother and left home in the middle of the night, Eddie started running behind them fast-ass girls from the clubs I forbade him to go to. He ended up getting that evil ass woman pregnant who stole all his savings before running off to DC. We had no clue if she or that baby survived, but by the grace of God, Devin found his way back to us. He and Yvonne here, my other greatest blessing."

A tear found its way down my cheek as I listened with focused intent at her story. It felt oddly nourishing hearing her out, that I couldn't help but ask. "How did Seymour die?"

Her eyes lingered on Vonnie as she said it. "Terrible farming accident. One Stevie and me never spoke about after she ran him over."

"Ran him...over?" I exclaim in disbelief, hoping I misheard her. "Surely granny didn't..."

"The dead tell no tales, baby. That's all I'll say about that. Besides, Stevie and I...became something meaningful after that. We bonded over so much tragedy that it felt so natural to take that step with her."

My brow crinkles as I consider the magnitude of her admission. But more curiosity was killing the cat, I supposed, as I eagerly awaited her to finish.

"Stephenie Gresham was the peace I always needed in all that pain. Same as Vonnie is to yours."

"Mine?" I questioned. My mouth widened at the realization of what she was saying, and my heart thundered in my chest.

"Wait." I started, turning fully to the kind old lady. "You and...Grandma Stevie?"

"Right again, Kimmy girl. She was the love of my life. The best partner a girl could ask for. I took care of her until her dying day and..." Her eyes squeeze shut. "That pain shakes up all my insides. I still wake up not believing she's gone. That I can't reach over and give her all the love she's taught me over the years."

I'm not sure if I was prepared for the weight of her admission. She and my late granny, my fiery grandmother who barely recognized us when we moved to Richmond, were involved in the longest secret affair I never knew about. A shiver runs its way up my spine, but not from disgust, but relief. It felt...good to know this piece of sensitive, sweet information about the grandmother I regretted never getting a chance to truly connect with. Talking about her like this so open and freely, and the knowledge that she and I had more in common gave me peace.

Like Vonnie did. The girl who visited all my dreams and left her love behind. If possible, my feelings intensified triple-fold for my unconscious love, and my heart ached at the thought of her remaining sleep.

"Vonnie's my peace, too." I breathed, watching Vonnie's heart monitor with a sobering futility. "What if she doesn't wake up? Doesn't come back to me? I don't know what I'd do if—"

"Shh," Mamma Dean croons, reaching over to wrap her arms around me. Despite my aversion to physical contact, her embrace is welcome as I collapse in her arms. "Have faith, baby. You still have a chance. Vonnie is still alive. Still right here with us. You tell her exactly how you feel every single day until she opens those eyes. You're what she needs. Just be there for her, honey."

"It hurts so bad..." I blubber, sobs wracking my chest and rocking us both.

"Your grandma saw those spirits, too."

"W-What?"

"Mmhm." She hums. "Everybody thought she was crazy when she'd say her dead momma visited her every Mother's Day, but I knew. I believed in her powers to connect with the other side. She told me her middle granddaughter had that same gift when you walked in her room on a Mother's Day and started up a conversation with her own late momma. You're special, girl. I know it. And whoever those spirits are that you were talking to when I came in here, you be sure to set boundaries. Let them know you mean business when it comes to Vonnie's healing, as well as your own. Free yourself."

"You knew the entire time that I saw spirits."

"Kind of. I just believed in the love of my life's sight. She knew, and believed it. So, I did, too."

"Free myself." I mutter, not really a question, but she answers anyway.

"Yes. Free yourself. And talk to Vonnie. You can't truly free her unless you forgive and free yourself, baby. Lay it all out. Be with her."

I chew on my lip as my eyes fix on my precious girl. My everything.

"Vonnie Carlson." I begin as I approach her bed to grab her clammy hand.

I said the words that felt the truest and closest to my heart since seeing her at that funeral. While I harbored guilt at neglecting my granny's going home ceremony, I couldn't deny the joy and heat that filled me at glancing at the girl with the large afro and black dress. Her brown eyes, through which I saw Michael, drew me in like a drug when I first saw them. And then I knew. Knew in my heart and soul that we belonged together. Like Mamma Dean and Grandma Stevie, she was the peace I knew and needed to heal. To learn to love every part of myself despite the hell that was my life. For her, I'd go on.

"Vonnie." I breathed again, another tear slipping past the barrier of my eyes and heart. "I love you."

17

BASEMENT

"Vonnie, want to walk Mommy somewhere?" Helen, my mother, asked as we strode down the littered streets of DC.

She, my twin brother Michael, and I were walking home from school and it was a cloudy foreboding day. Almost as foreboding as the dark circles that lined Mommy's sunken eyes.

I stared up at her, confused. "Where?"

She made a point to avoid my eyes. "To a friend's house. For a favor."

At the mention of that haunting word, my blood chilled. I knew what this meant and I dreaded whatever this favor entailed this time.

"What friend?" Mikey cut in, his usual exuberant chattiness bursting to the surface as it always did. "And can I come, too?"

When no answer came from her, Mikey persisted, much against the warning look I shot him.

"Mommy? Did you hear me? I want to come with you guys!" He chirped; a small frown marred his chubby face.

Without warning, Mommy stopped. I paused a little ways behind them, but Mikey seemed not to notice Mommy's lack of footsteps behind him.

"Michael." She bit out.

He froze, the catchy nursery rhyme we learned in school that day silencing in his throat. "Yes, mommy?"

"What did I tell you about interfering?" Her tone was gentle, yet laden with menacing promise.

Mikey faced her, his eyes tinged with fear and a brazenness I wished I'd inherited. "You said not ever interfere with favors."

"And what else?" She goaded, slinking closer to him.

"Um," he hesitated, thinking. "Never ask questions. Ever."

Mommy's smile was like slow pouring acid as it twisted her face and promised danger. She knelt down before him and spoke to him softly, cupping his face. "Good boy. You remember the way home?"

"Home?!" He screeched, distraught as his eyes bounced between her and me. "No! I-I wanna go with Vonnie."

Instinctively, I squeezed my eyes shut. I knew what would happen whenever Mommy's limits were pushed. Tested. Especially by one of us.

I didn't see it, but heard the contact of flesh against flesh, intuiting the slap she delivered like clockwork.

"Mommy!" Mikey screamed again in frustration.

I opened my eyes again to bear witness to Mommy smack him again, regardless of the unwanted attention her actions garnered in broad daylight.

"No. Fucking. Questions." She growled, shaking his meek shoulders. "Look at me. Tell me you understand."

Mikey shook his head, his eyes trained only on me. There was a fierce resolve behind my little brother's stare, one I'd only seen when he was talking about dinosaurs.

"No!" He seethed, real close to her face. "Take me. Take me instead. Leave Vonnie alone!"

Another smack, before she snarled. "Mikey, you got one more time to—"

"Mikey!" I blubbered, hating how all this went so wrong so fast. My entire body trembled in fear and my little voice was no more than a squeak from underuse. I didn't speak. Everybody knew, Mikey was the voice between the two of us, and I kept quiet as much as possible. I knew what kind of trouble talking could get you into. I knew it all too well.

"Please..." I whispered brokenly. "I can do it. I'm okay!"

"Vonnie!" He shouted, fighting in Mommy's ironclad hold. "Get off of me, Mom!"

"Just...I'll..." I stuttered, unknowing the best words for the situation. My tongue often got tied like this.

Hating my uselessness, I turned and ran. Ran so far, and so long that my lungs protested against the sudden exertion.

"Vonnie!" Mommy called, and I could hear her running after me.

If I kept running, then the trouble wouldn't come. I wouldn't be the cause of hurting Mikey anymore. So, I kept running despite the frantic screams from my twin and mom that evening.

"Vonnie, come back!" Mikey hollers behind me somewhere.

"Come back, you little bitch!" Mommy's screams are drawing closer and closer to me, and my legs are aching at this point. I'm so out of breath but need to keep going. Keep running away from her mean words and Mikey's evident pain until it all stops. My chest twists in pain when I trip over a protruding piece of concrete in the sidewalk, causing me to tumble over into the ground.

The blow knocked the wind out of me and stole my voice, making all that came out a tortured moan.

The footsteps got louder, closer, and I closed my eyes to prepare for the worst. It was her.

"Don't you run from me again, girl." She demands, winded.

I keep my face buried into the ground, not bothering to answer.

A forceful yank of my ponytail forces my head back. "Understand?" She bites out.

"O-Okay!" I gasp, my scalp burning under the exertion of her grip in my thick hair. The trickle traveling through my scalp following the agonizing pain of her actions made me groan from the bruises I'd have to address later on.

The sky is turning an ominous dark as the shadows reach the dark corners in the alleyways a feet from where we stand. Well, Mommy is standing over my vertical body on the ground as I inwardly block out her insults and pray to be somewhere else. Anywhere else.

"Shit, it's getting late. Let's go." She grumbled, pulling my backpack forcefully until I'm upright. She's practically dragging me down the desolate, littered streets and a terrifying thought comes to me.

"Where's Mikey?" I asked, keeping my voice small and non-threatening so as not to set her off again. My knees and scalp took enough of a beating for one evening.

"Fuck if I know. I guess he went back to the house." She grunts, her tone edgy and unfocused.

I'm beyond scared and mortified by this, because there was just no way he'd leave me alone with her. When he walked in on one of her "favors" leaving our bedroom after returning from a playdate with Devin last month, things changed. I never expressed the true nature of what Mommy's favors entailed, but I always knew that he knew the truth. Since then, it was a rare event for me to be alone with our mom in the daytime, seeing as Mikey always had "something he had to show me," or a playdate he begged our parents that I tag along with. His friends, who were privileged boys we went to school with, often complained when Mikey dragged me to the playdates, but deep down inside I knew. Knew he did his best to keep her away from me. Whenever Devin went to his friend Kale's house in the burbs, Mikey would practically plead with our big brother to take us along when daddy went on business runs for the laundromat. The thing we feared the most that we never shared outwardly to each other? Being left alone in the house with Her. Lucy. The Evil. Mommy.

I gulp the following questions down about Mikey's whereabouts, knowing all too well that I'd be met with either a curse or the back of her hand.

We entered a familiar neighborhood, one that seemed to spark more of my confusion as we stopped in front of the large white colonial with immaculate gardening. I recognized this house, the one my big brother often allowed Mikey and me to accompany him after school some days. My mind flickers to the image of Kale, the dark-haired boy with ocean blue eyes. He and Devin sometimes hung out and played video games together in Kale's humungous bedroom. I wasn't quite sure what his parents did for work, but their huge modern colonial home could easily swallow our itty-bitty craftsman.

I shimmy out of her tight hold to stare up at her. Her eyes are all over the place as she craned her neck to peer into the back yard area. The bugs in the night created an eerie cricketing as we stood there.

"Is Devin here?" I asked, a little perturbed by my lack of knowledge on this information. Whenever Devin left to hang out with Kale, he told both Mikey and me, in case we wanted to tag along, which was always.

"Shut up." She growled, still glancing around as if expecting someone.

"Are we picking him up?"

"Girl!" She hissed, turning her death glare on me. "If you don't stop asking me all these questions..."

"I'm sorry." I mutter, looking away in fear and guilt.

I wasn't usually this chatty, but a weird sensation formed in my chest and gut as we stood there. Call it intuition, but I felt death that night before it happened. Before death happened this night and our family broke permanently into untenable pieces.

"Aye!" A male's voice hums in the night air. It's coming from the side of the house, I notice, since Mommy looks in its direction, too.

A huge, genuine smile, one I'd never seen directed at me, curves her lips and for once, in that single moment, she's beautiful. Beautiful despite the bruises on her forearms and shadows under her eyes. That smile rejuvenates her, making her look like a slightly older, happier version of me instead of her usual grouchy, exhausted self.

"Come on!" She sings excitedly as she grabs my arm. My legs move out of numb curiosity and latent panic, but my mouth drops at what I see when we reach the back door.

Or, rather, who *I see.*

"How are ya, love?" Kale's dad, Cliff greets us warmly as we stand before him.

"Mr. Cliff?" I breathe in astonishment.

I knew Kale's daddy, a tall, kind man with a funny accent, insisted we call him Uncle Cliff. But only when Kale's mommy wasn't around. I think he was some kind of scientist, since he'd often led us to the downstairs office where empty beakers and bottles lay around. He and Mikey had a particular bond, since they both shared a love of science, and would often disappear in the office or kitchen together when the three of us would visit.

Mommy's smile brightens. "Yeah, wassup. You got the stuff like you said?"

He gave a tight, single nod but looked at me. "We have all the time in the world to discuss it, Helen. Come inside and relax a little."

"No!" *she snarled, her smile fading into tight lipped anger.* "I got to get home before my husband gets back and notices we missing. Come on, just give me the stuff like we agreed on."

"Helen." *He says, his tone gentle but warning, but his eyes never leave me. The attention makes me squirm.* "You're upsetting your precious daughter here?"

She flexes her jaw and crosses her arms. "This supposed to be a quick thing. In and out."

Sighing, he kneels down to study me. "Looks like your mummy gets cranky without her drugs, eh?"

I widened my eyes in shock. "Drugs?"

"Shit, Cliff!" *Mommy scolds before turning to me.* "Don't listen to him, Vonnie."

I stare between them, not sure who to trust but afraid all the same. "My mommy is sick, Mr. Cliff."

"Ah, ah, ah." *He tuts gently while wagging a chastising finger.* "What did I tell you to call me, Yvonne?"

I gulp again, retreating a step. "U-Uncle."

"Uncle who?"

"Uncle Cliff?"

"Good girl." He praises, giving my body an insipid once over before standing to his full six-foot height. "Now let's go inside before the neighbors catch wind of what we're up to."

"Is Devin here?" I blurt the question before I realize it and cup hands over my mouth.

They continue conversing like I never asked anyway.

Mommy sighs, rubbing her face. "I ain't going in there. But I got the money. Just give me what we talked about and we out."

"You got the full amount? The full Benjamin?"

A hundred dollars, I surmised, since we just finished a currency lesson in class last week. Why would he need a hundred dollars from her?

I peer up at her with the unasked question in my eyes. She bites her lip before fishing out a wad of cash from her bra.

He takes it, observing the wad with predatory focus. Then he frowns. Cold blue eyes glower into Mommy's face, who's averting her gaze away.

"Where's the rest of it?" He demands, his tone low, and controlled, but colder than before. "I told you to bring a Benjamin. This is less than half that."

"I know, I know!" She responds desperately, holding her hands up. "I remember the price we talked about yesterday. I just haven't been able to get the rest of it from Quincy since—"

"Hey." Uncle Cliff interrupts. "Come here."

"Why?" she counters, shifting from foot-to-foot nervously.

"Come. Here." He growls.

"Y-Yes, sir." She steps forward until her chest nearly touches his.

"What did I tell you about short changing me, huh?" His tone is controlled and still low, but less restrained than before. "I only produce top of the line grade. I have people from gangs to corporate company members who buy my product. And then there's you. You still owe me from the last time I spotted you."

"N-No!" she mews, weeping now. "I paid you last time!"

He chuckles before casting a disgusted look her way. "You think that tired roll in the sack was payment? Even if that sour pussy was enough to get me off for one night, it'd never be enough to erase that debt from last time. I'll ask you one more time, Helen: Where's. My. Money?"

She sank to her knees, sobbing and pleading out of control as she wrapped her arms around his long legs. "Cliff, please! You know my husband cut me off. This is all I got in the world. Please just give me one more taste. Just one..."

He studied his watch as if he'd rather be anywhere else than negotiating a drug deal in his backyard. "Perhaps we can work something out."

"Thank god, bless you!" She sighed in utter relief, like she just heard the greatest news in the world. *"I'll do anything. Want me to go back to your office like last time? I can make you feel good..."*

"Nope." He answered, cold and clipped before looking at my shocked expression. A smile curls his lips. *"Not you. But she can."*

"What?" Mommy and me gasp at the same time.

"Cliff?" She said, rising to her feet. *"For real?"*

He nods, a sinister smile on his face. *"I don't joke. Ever."*

"Okay..." she says, her voice distant as she considers something.

"Mommy, I don't want to go with him." I say pleadingly, my feet frozen to the earth as I watched him watch me.

She stares into my eyes for a long moment before answering. *"Nah."*

Relief floods my being at her words, and I clutch my heart to contain myself.

"You're telling me no?"

"Yeah, I am." She retorts, staring him in the eye a little more boldly. *"You can't have her. Not for free."*

"No!" I groaned in horror. It's my turn to collapse onto the ground, except it's her I'm hugging and begging for dear life to care. To please, just this once, give a fuck about her only daughter.

She shakes her leg to ward me off, and I fall to the ground again, crashing onto all my sore spots from when I tripped previously.

"Please..." I'm still begging, begging her to see me. To just look at me for real and find an ounce of affection to spare me from this.

She addresses Uncle Cliff. "That's why I brought her, after all. For insurance."

"Insurance?" He questions, taken aback. "You do realize you're in no position to make demands. You owe me money."

"I know. You can have her for the night."

"Absolutely not."

"But I thought you wanted her?"

Uncle Cliff examines me on the ground, his eyes a blue storm of confliction. "How much?" He asks, his jaw tight with frustration from the power shift in the conversation.

Mommy smiles wickedly. "A bag. No, two. Two bags for an hour with her."

He laughs, shifting his weight. "Do I look stupid? Two bags for only an hour? If it's two bags you want, then she'll need to at least stay the night."

"Deal." She agrees, a little too quickly, and I notice that same youthful smile return as they shake on it. "Now gimme the bag!"

"Settle down, eh? I'll need to go and get it from the basement."

"Whatever, just hurry up!" She spits before he disappears into the house.

Hot tears stream down my face at the realization of what just happened. I didn't know what Uncle Cliff wanted with me, but my gut told me it was something evil. Something dirty. Something that'd break me for all of time.

A cold quiet crackles between us now that we're alone. I'm sobbing so hard at this point that my body is trembling on the ground.

"Vonnie, I'll be back to get you in the morning, okay?" Her voice is soft, like when she comes to collect a night "favor," and a tad bit of calm storms me. But it's a pseudo contentedness, because she adds, "Remember not to tell daddy, okay? Or Mikey or Devin. This favor stays between us girls."

Her hand is on my trembling shoulders. "Okay, baby? Remember this is for my treatment. I need this. You're mommy's savior, you know?"

Her voice is so soothing and maternal that I want to believe them. I want to trust in her ability to love me. Maybe this was for the best, I thought. Since she was sick, was I being selfish by denying her this one medicine dose? That familiar wave of numb submission surges through me, and I find myself nodding. Not in *agreement, but an automatic action my neck's gotten used to after she gentles her voice to ask a favor. Stay small, I thought, sink inside and bury further into the darkness to get through this. Because mommy's got her own darkness, I realize, and it's so encompassing that it blinds her from truly seeing me. She doesn't truly see me in all that darkness and I often preferred to stay hidden.*

"Vonnie!" A voice hollers in the distance. The voice is winded, but familiar. Dare I hope? Hope that this voice was my salvation in all this darkness. I almost think I'm hallucinating, but dismiss that thought when Mommy stands and faces the voice.

"Mikey?" She queries, truly surprised.

I sit up and see him. My brave, winded, twin brother who's keeled over in an attempt to catch his breath.

"Didn't I tell you to go home?" She barks.

"Vonnie..." he pants, "...are...you...okay?"

I shake my head, more tears spilling as I croak.

Mommy yanks me upright and drags me over to stand in front of Mikey. "Go. Home. Now."

"Mommy, stop it!" Mikey complains, his voice hard yet desperate. "I followed y'all. Just punish me instead. I did a bad thing."

"Fuck, Michael, you never listen to me!" She hisses in his face.

Mikey ignores her. "Vonnie, are you okay? Do you hurt anywhere?"

I'm too scared to respond.

Mikey walks over and shakes my shoulders. "Damn it, Vonnie, talk to me! Use your voice. Are you hurt?"

My lips tremble, but still no sound comes out as I stare into his identically brown eyes.

He grabs my hand. "Come on. Let's go home. We'll tell Devin. He'll know what to do."

"Oh, hell no!" Mommy screeches, forcing the two of us apart and holding each of our hands in hers. She's dragging us to the back of the house, where the deal took place, and my heart drops when Uncle Cliff steps back out into the yard.

"Well, well." he said excitedly. "Who do we have here? Is that my little Paleontologist?"

Mikey glares at him, hard. "What's my sister doing here, huh?"

I think I saw Uncle Cliff's cheeks turn pink as he kneels in front of Mikey. He's carrying a black shopping bag in his hands.

"You know. I'm still working on that tadpole experiment in my lab if you want to see, Michael."

Mikey's eyes light up for a moment, then harden the next. "No, thank you. I want to go home."

"But it's a really good experiment..."

Mikey yanks against our mother's hand. "No! Just let us go home! I heard what y'all were talking about when I ran up."

Cliff raises his brows, intrigued. "Did you?"

If I could go back, I'd tell my brother not to do it. To do the thing that seals our fate into that basement that night. But I can't work miracles. Could only watch as Mikey gargled for a long moment before spitting in his face.

"Fuck you."

Cliff laughs maniacally as he wipes off the wad of spit on his brow. He stands up, concentrating a sinister smile on my brother.

"Two nights." he states, glancing at us both. "Give me two nights. With both of them."

Mommy didn't hesitate. "How much you willing to pay?"

"I'll get you three bags of high grade. Enough to keep you high for weeks—"

"Done!" she mumbles, pushing us into the arms of the strong man. He squeezes us tightly into his arms.

We're both struggling to get free when he whispers, "You'll see some familiar faces down there. Trust me. It'll be a party. A playdate."

Mommy's salivating as she dances with the black bag in her hands. "Mm mm! I'll, uh, be back to come get y'all after Uncle Cliff is done."

"Done what?" My brother rasps as he thrashes. "Don't do this!"

Mommy's already walking towards the front yard by the time Mikey screams, "Just take Vonnie! Mom! Take Vonnie! Take Vonnie! Take her away from here!"

His words hang empty in the air as she disappears down the street.

"Shut your fucking blubbering! You little shit!" Cliff demands as he wrestles us through the kitchen and down some steps.

We're in the lower ground, a basement, and the sight of two other classmates makes me cower in fright. There's a huge bathtub in the corner and a cage in the room. One of the girl's is in that cage, her eyes are half open as she looks at us, as if she wants to sit up but can't. There's another body on a raised table in the room...and she's still. Eerily pale and motionless under the harsh hanging lamp. I stop fighting, knowing it's useless and accepting my fate, but Mikey doesn't get the memo.

"Ouch!" Cliff shrieks, and I see my brother sink his teeth into his meaty arm before dropping us.

I hit the concrete floor with a hard thunk, and he's raining punches on Mikey. Out of the corner of my eye, I see a room. Terrified and pushing it, I crawl over to it. Praying it's a door to freedom and salvation from this monster.

But it isn't.

It's a closet, empty and large enough for me to get inside and shut it behind me. All I hear is Cliff cursing and Mikey groaning. There's splashing, too, but I'm sure I'm imagining that. Sure, this will all be over soon. Sure, that the scream isn't really my brother yelling, "Yvonne!" before a gurgling noise fills the putrid air.

It isn't real. Heavens, no, it couldn't be real. I chant this over and over, my eyes shut and heart caving in. Before the darkness can envelop the rest of me, the little of me that's left, I open my eyes.

18

CAUGHT ME BREATHING

The familiar sounds of gunshots penetrate the darkness, and a sliver of light nearly pierces me from its intensity. My eyes are so dry it feels like bags of sand weigh them down. The dryness of my throat nearly strangles me when I open my mouth to try speaking. It hurts. Bad.

After several blinks that eat up all my energy and take all my effort a shrill scream accompanies the familiar sounds in the room. A room.

I'm in a room.

"Vonnie? Sweetie, you're awake!" She squeals.

I fight to keep my strained eyes open despite the crust in them. I am, indeed, inside a room, but not the dingy closet in that basement. There's nothing here to indicate the black nothingness of the Mind Mansion, either. Last I remembered was Mikey's voice and being sucked into one of those rooms.

A girl runs over to me, her red hair is like a cloud of fire as she hovers and stares into my sore eyes.

"Baby, you're awake? Oh my god, I didn't think you'd ever…" Her morose voice trails off, and I detect the tears falling from her green eyes.

Her hand reaches out for mine, which is tucked into the side of the bed beside my hip.

"I miss you. I believed in you. Knew you would come back to me." She kisses my hand, and I note the contrast between her cold hands and warm lips.

I open my mouth to address her, to reassure her that I'm fine, when she jumps up. "Fuck, what am I doing? I got to tell Mamma Dean!"

"Hey…" I rasp, but she's already gone.

I right myself, turning to study the large room. A beanbag chair is situated near the flat screen TV where multicolor game controllers are sprawled on the floor. Judging from the large space gun the blue alien's equipped with, *Weapons from Zeldar 3* is paused on the screen. Was she playing my video game while I napped?

She comes back into the room with an older lady in tow. The elderly woman is cradling a mocha skinned infant and wearing a yellow track suit with a box braid wig I recognized from earlier.

"Praise God!" she calls, doubling over slightly while clutching a weathered hand to her large chest. "Thank you for breathing life back into my grandbaby. Thank you for bringing her back home." Her legs buckle and head arches back, and I see the tears sliding down her face as she does a praise dance with the wide-eyed baby staring up at her.

The redhead girl joins her, but her moves are much more measured and awkward.

"Mamma Dean?" I inquire, relieved for the sound to finally come through my throat.

They both pause, as does the mixture of laugh-tears that fill the air, to look at me.

"Vonnie, baby, you feeling okay?" Mamma Dean asks beside my bed. Her hand touches my forehead. "No fever. You don't look pale anymore either. Thank you, Jesus."

I struggle to move my neck, but soon find myself nodding. "I feel fine. Just took a quick nap. But I'm up now. And...hungry."

"No problem, baby. I'll get you some smoked ribs." Mamma Dean chortles as she sits in the chair near my bed. She sobers all of a sudden. "But honey you wasn't napping. You've been asleep for a while."

"A while?"

"Yes." She says, looking at the girl.

The girl stares at me, a sad smile on her face. "You've been sleeping for three weeks. A coma, actually. I'm so sorry."

I return her stare blankly, not quite comprehending her words. Not understanding the seriousness of what she just told me. Surely, she was mistaken. It was only a nap...

"No. No. This isn't right. I just dozed off for a minute."

The redheaded girl chews on her lip and fidgets with the hem of her white tee shirt. The tee has the words 'Free Krimzon' embroidered on it, and I recall the *Weapons from Zeldar's* alien hero as well as the fanfic conference I won it from.

"And why are you wearing my clothes?" I say, harsher than intended, which makes her fidget more. "And playing my games? Your mama teach you manners? Since that's not the way to introduce yourself to people you've never met."

Confusion roils through me as I observe their jaws drop.

Mamma Dean speaks up. "Uh, Vonnie? What you talking about, baby? This is Kimmy– ain't no stranger."

I frown at the old lady. "Who's Kimmy?"

'Kimmy' gasps and cups a hand over her mouth. "Stop playing, Yvonne. You know me."

"Um..." I utter while giving her slender body a onceover. I recognize several things: the alien tee shirt of mine she's wearing as well as the royal blue gym shorts I wore all the time. Other than the stolen attire, there isn't much about her identity I recognize.

"There's been a lot of changes since you've been asleep, baby." Mamma Dean mutters apologetically. "Give her some time to get readjusted, Kimmy."

"Yvonne." She whimpers, drawing nearer with hesitant steps. "You remember me. I know you do."

I squint at her to piece together meaning and familiarity. But it doesn't come.

"Ma'am, I'm sorry. Whoever you're expecting can't be me. I literally have never seen you before."

"No!" she groans, dropping to her knees to grab my hand in hers with a pleading look on her face.

"You know me. Remember me, your number one fan. The lake. The spirits. Mikey?"

"Mikey?" I demand, yanking my hand out of hers, and unclear why that motion brings immediate sorrow to my soul. "How do you know that name? Are you some kind of stalker?"

"Babe..." she whimpers again, tears steady and streaming as she attempts to reach out for me again. "I see you. I see you. Think real hard."

I set my gaze on her for a long moment. "I can see you, too. Can you please go stand over there or something?"

She does me one better. Sniffling, she stands up to dash out of the room emitting the most pitiful cries as she stomps downstairs.

I gawk at Mamma Dean, who's pursing her lips with a regretful expression.

"She's been with you the entire time, you know?"

I sigh my aggravation, "Right."

"No, really. She's been bogarting your room, giving you baths, and protecting you from unwanted company. She even been playing your little video games hoping the sounds would maybe wake you up."

"What? Really?"

She nods. "Played that space game over and over. Lord knows I'm sick of that damn silly music."

I giggled unconsciously, sinking deeper into the bed as guilt from her words hit me. "Did something happen? Why was I in a coma? Did she do something to me or maybe I fell?"

"No, baby." She responds gravely, her eyes somber. "I think you had another one of them fits, except, you didn't come back this time. Kimmy found you up in that guest room unconscious. God, and the look you had on your face..."

"I know, Mamma Dean." I whispered brokenly. "I'm here. I'm back. I promise not to worry you like that again."

"Good."

"Oh, and whose baby is that?"

She peers down at the baby with mild surprise, as if she's just realizing there's a whole human glued to her ample bosom.

"Oh, uh, this here is...Romelo."

"Romelo?" I wracked my mind, attempting to place familiarity to that name. Again, nothing comes. I adjust myself, careful not to yank too hard at the tubes in my arm. "Somebody's kid from church?"

She purses her lip and averts her eyes. "Vonnie, there's a lot that went on while you were asleep. Lots of change."

"Change? Like what?"

"You really did wake up!" A deep voice exclaimed from the door. Three tall men enter the room, each of their complexions of varying shades of brown. One is insanely tall; his honey brown skin and short curls reveal his mixed heritage. Bone Alvarez. Yes, I recognize my good friend instantly as well as his signature six-foot six towering height.

The shortest one with the darkest skin is mouthwateringly handsome in his beater and blue jeans. Malik Hinton, my other homie and typical basketball teammate.

Then there's the guy with sorrowful eyes who makes my heart race from anxiety. He sort of sulks inside slightly behind the others, since Bone and Malik are all up in my face in seconds upon their arrival.

"*iDios*," Bone breathes, peering worriedly into my eyes and examining my face for obvious health issues, I assumed, since his stare was filled with medical focus. "Saw Kimmy run outta here saying you were awake. What happened to you, man?"

"You really had us scared." Malik chimed in, eyeing me, too. "And I ain't no bitch, but I was like, real scared you weren't gonna wake up."

"Watch your mouth." Mamma Dean warns. And I catch her bouncing the fussy baby in her arms.

Malik grinned sheepishly, rubbing his neck. "My bad, Mamma Dean."

I tentatively try to sit upright, when the world spins and I'm forced to sink back down.

"Hey, hey." Zay cautions as he cuts through the two guys beside my bed. His hands are on my shoulders, and I find it hard to not notice the bags under his eyes. "Just relax. Take it easy, Von."

"Zay." I whispered, emotion overtaking me.

"We'll talk later, okay?" He said, seeming to respond to my unspoken question about before. He turns to Mamma Dean with troubled eyes. "Mamma, you tell her yet? Bout the baby and stuff?"

A tight, forced smile makes it way to my granny's face as she returns his worried look. "I was getting to it, Zay. Was trying to give her some time to adjust."

"Adjust to what?" I inquired, suspicious now. It felt like there was something in the ether, just within reach but not quite close enough to allow me to grasp its meaning. "What?"

Zay casts me a weary gaze. "Just relax, okay?"

"I am relaxed! Now what's up?"

"Vonnie, just calm down—" Mamma Dean starts.

"I am fine! Stop gentle-talking me and tell me what is happening? Does it have something to do with the redhead girl?"

I'm only cognizant that I'm shouting because of the resounding cries that erupt from the baby, Romelo. His face turns several shades of pink from frustration and fright, and it makes me want to kick myself.

"Sorry." I muttered to the room full of curious watchers.

Zay opened his mouth to say something to me when another voice took its place from the hall.

"Mamma Dean, I got the bottle!" The man said, rushing inside the room wearing a white tee and yellow gym shorts. His hair is buzzed close and he's rocking a beard. Even though his appearance has changed with time and circumstance, I recognize that face and voice anywhere. It's him.

The voice of my protector and favorite person.

"Why's everybody in here—" He begins to ask but drops the bottle and his jaw when he gets a look at me. "Vonnie? Baby, are you awake?"

I nod, tears streaming down my face as the memories rush back. And I mean, a ton of memories.

There's a lake, the picture is fuzzy, but I'm suddenly picturing the small body of water and a cool breeze. Tears roll down my eyes from the loneliness, from the feeling of being so unwanted and forlorn. I was sick of roaming, and wanted a home I could be proud of. Mikey is with me, I feel him, like always in my mind and heart, but there's someone else that materializes. Her scent is a forbidden fruit, a combination of berries and musk, making me inhale as I turn to the source. It's her. I see...her. The girl, no, woman, with red hair and pale skin. Her green eyes glitter under the evening moonlight and I find myself walking into her open arms. I know her. I know her. This was—

His arms are around me in a second, and I feel the sobs shaking his hard body as I bury my face in his chest.

"God, baby girl, don't scare me like that again. You hear me?"

It's Devin, my one and only brother who left me four years ago to enlist. I hadn't seen nor heard from him since deploying, and the sudden rush of images flashing before my eyes nearly made me faint again.

"Devin..." I whimper, as the scene of his departure plays on repeat in my head. "How are you here? When did you get here?"

"Last week." He chokes out, still fighting for control of his emotions, no doubt. "I got here and was looking for you all over the farm. Then Mamma Dean told me you was..."

"Yeah." I grunt. "I know. Sorry."

"Sorry for what? You ain't ask to have a seizure or sleep for three weeks. It's all right. I'm here now. Back for good."

I peered up at him with misty eyes. "Really?"

He nodded, pulling me back into his embrace. "I'm just glad you're okay. You're back with me."

Somewhere in the background, a baby's cries could be heard. Blinking, I realize the situation, that there was a wailing, unidentified child in Mamma Dean's arms.

"He is fussin mighty hard." Mamma Dean complained, bouncing him and humming her church hymns. "Devin, please come settle your son."

"All right." He agreed as he pulled away to stand up. Once the baby was in his arms, true to her word, he calmed. In fact, his giggles were infectious as I found myself smiling at him.

"You...have a son?"

"Yes. He's five months old." He bounces the baby on his right side and says, "Rome, this is your Aunt Vonnie."

He buries his face into Devin's chest, and I can't help but point out the obvious truth that makes my heart ache.

"He looks just like me." I say behind tears and reach for him. I'm not sure how I didn't notice his similarly chubby brown cheeks and slightly curved eyes like mine.

"Romelo Michael Carlson, is what we named him." Devin adds before placing the shy infant in my arms.

He settles in my arms like he belonged, and my heart just thuds from the amount of emotion that wells up in me.

"Michael? Y'all named him Michael?"

He nodded, a proud smile on his face. "Sure did. Had to name him after the best brother we'd ever had."

"Aww. Hi, Romelo Michael." I breathe to the baby who's smiling back at me. "Where's his mother? She here, too?"

"No." Devin answered quickly, cold and clipped. "She's dead. It's just us."

"I'm sorry, bro."

He shrugged. "No sweat. But I want to run something by you, sis."

"Sure."

"How would you feel about coming to live with me?"

"Um...what?"

"I got a place in town. It's a small house I'm renting, and I know you love it here at Mamma Dean's, but I just thought I would come and offer it to you. I'm sorry it took so long, but it's the home we'd always talked about getting. Just us."

"Dev, I don't know what to say." I uttered, kind of speechless.

"Told him you'd want to stay here. With family. On the farm." Mama Dean interrupts indignantly.

I allowed the idea room in my head to dwell. This was my dream when we lived under Lucy's rule and when I occupied that cramped basement closet fearing death. The promise I made to myself and Mikey was to settle home, and home was always where my brother was, but...

I shake my head. "Can I think about it?"

He smiles. "Of course. We'll table it for now and I'll give you some room to adjust."

"Thanks."

"You boys ought to get going, now." Mamma Dean addresses the crowd of men still in the room observing us. "It's getting late and Vonnie's doctor is on the way to check on her."

Malik raises his hand.

Mamma Dean waves him away humorously. "Boy you play too much raising your hand like I'm some teacher. What you want?"

His eyes skid around the room before resettling back on her. "I smell them ribs you cooking in the back. Can I stay for dinner?"

She chuckles as they begin towards the door. "Y'all is family. Course you can stay. Everybody gets ribs tonight since we celebrate my grandbaby waking up! Praise Jesus!"

They clamor out of the door, but not before I rear up and yell. "Hey! You guys!"

Malik, Bone, and Zay scuffle into my room.

"What? What's wrong?" Zay growls.

"You okay, you feel faint?" Bone asks.

I shake my head, grinning and grateful for my overbearing homies who were the best brothers a girl could have.

"I'm fine, but there's something I need to do. Mind helping me out?"

19

SOUL TO KEEP

Minutes later, the guys helped me down the steps. I'm mostly being carried as we walk through the large farmhouse where Mamma Dean shoots us a confused stare.

"Where y'all going? And why is she up?"

Zay answers, "We taking her outside for some air. Just to the front porch, not far."

"All right." She grumbles. "But make sure she's back in bed in an hour. No discussions."

"Yes, ma'am." We all mumble in sync to the loving old lady.

Once we're outside, I scan the porch and front yard. "Where is she?"

"Hmm," Bone hums curiously. "She was just out here. Last time I saw her was on the porch crying."

"Fuck..." I scoff, inwardly hating myself for making my girl upset. I asked the guys to help me outside to speak with her. To tell her I remembered her, and us, and to reassure her of my love. I needed to see her. Now.

"Where could she be?" Malik asked.

"I don't know." Says Zay.

A thought hits me, and I intuit her location the same as I did when I unconsciously found myself at her guest bedroom door that night the darkness took me.

"She's at the lake." I stated, and the guys share confused gazes.

"The lake? On Aunt Stevie's land?" Malik inquired like I was crazy for mentioning it. "You sure?"

I nodded.

"Well, let's take the truck. We'll get you there, Von." Zay, my favorite homie, cut in as he escorted us to the old Jeep parked out front.

While the drive was usually a short one, it felt like the longest three minutes of my life. I'm not all the way sure why my encounter with Devin forced the memories back into me, but I'm grateful. I couldn't explain the emotion that lived in me when I could no longer recognize Kimmy after waking up. Staring at her felt like a latent wave of anxiety threatening to drown me if looking too closely. After seeing her run out of the room crying, the feeling was easy to identify as it cracked the previously soft parts of my heart.

Guilt. Emptiness, and so much guilt.

I wait for the familiar voice to reassure me, to let me know that all my wrongdoings were sane and redeemable, but it doesn't come. Another wave of pain awash my insides in crippling agony as I remembered what happened before passing out. Mikey left. He left me with promises to return, but as I closed my eyes to search for him, his presence was no longer there. Gone, like he'd never been there in the first place to guide me to my sweet Kimmy.

"Von, you all right?" It was Zay. His light brown eyes flicker between me and the road as we pull onto the dirt road nearest the lake clearing.

I wiped my eyes. "Yeah, yeah. I'm good. Just happy to be alive."

He eyed me suspiciously, and I could tell he sensed the lie since he knew me so well, but was glad he played it off. "Just take it easy, okay?"

"I will."

"You better." He chuffs while exiting the truck. Once he's at my door, he opens it and extends his hand to me. "Milady?"

I laughed wryly at that and grabbed it. "Shut up, man."

Bone spoke from the backseat he occupied next to Malik. "I don't know what you said to Kimmy, but you better be nice!"

"For real, man." Malik cut in disapprovingly. "She held it down for you while you was out. She the real MVP for that."

"Word up." Zay finished in his familiar Yankee accent once he helped me out of the truck.

I scrutinized them all with a glare I kept on reserve for these guys whenever they ganged up on me. Like now.

"Okay, okay." I muttered before turning around. I scanned the open clearing that existed just before the lake, searching desperately for her. My heart did anxious leaps in my chest when I could not find her and I nearly doubted my intuition before I saw her.

Her red hair billowed easily in the chilly Richmond air and her back was turned to me. She was still dressed in my alien shirt and shorts, and I cursed under my breath for how I spat the ugly words at her about it. After pitching the guys a quick conciliatory nod, I started for her on unsure legs. These legs hadn't been used in three weeks, and they'd be limp string beans if it wasn't for my green-eyed girl's efforts to keep them stretched while I slept. While we hadn't known each other long, so many aspects of her character shined through these past few weeks. According to Mamma Dean, she slept in the same room as me and made sure I stretched, ate, and breathed regularly. She adopted nearly every aspect of my healthcare responsibilities, and the mere image of her beside my bed each day sent pangs of guilt and adoration to my chest. I loved her so much it hurt, and after losing Mikey for the second time I knew this new problem had to be solved one way, and one way only.

"Keep using that beautiful voice of yours..."

My little brother's final words nearly tore me in half as I limped closer to the love of my life and the scariest thing I'd ever do.

The crunch of leaves under my feet caused her to turn fretful green eyes in my direction.

"Yvonne!" She demanded with breathless relief while clutching her chest. "What the hell are you doing out of bed?"

She reached out to feel my forehead after standing and closing the gap between us. In one quick movement, I grabbed her wrist to pull her into my arms. Tears streamed down my face before I could catch them and the normal consideration I left on reserve for her dissipated into relentless need. A raw desperation to make her feel my next words instead of just listening.

She wrapped her arms around me. "Yvonne? You're shaking. Are you all right?"

"I'm the biggest piece of shit for treating you like that. For always letting my mind dictate what my heart wants instead of just feeling. I am so...so sorry. Please forgive me."

"Yvonne." She choked out, digging her nails into my back by the ferocity of her embrace. "Please try to calm down. Being this upset can't be good for your health right now."

I took a deep breath, praying it did a little something in mollifying my stormy soul and quaking body. It did.

"That's better." She whispered in an airy sing-song breath that lifted my spirits instantly before pulling away slightly to stare into my eyes. "Now, tell me what you're doing here."

I nodded, never breaking eye contact with her. "I'm here for you. For us. Like it should've been from the start. When I saw you at Aunt Stevie's funeral there was something about the way you looked at me that awakened a part of me I thought died in that closet. Died with my brother and any sense of safety I'd ever felt."

She shook her head. "Yvonne, no. I won't do this with you."

"Please just hear me out. Please?"

Her eyes seemed to twinkle under the moonlight overhead and the site took my breath away. I couldn't help but caress her face as I continued.

"I want us to break this cycle of hurting each other. Of violating each other. I don't want you to ever feel like you don't want to be here with me. I just came out here to give you my word."

She frowned. "What's that?"

"I want us to start slow. Date and get to know the barest parts of each other. The sides we don't let anyone else see. I thought about it a lot, and knew it was you I wanted to allow inside."

"Inside the Mind Mansion?" She asked, her tone wavering.

I shook my head fiercely at that. "God, no! Don't you see? That place is...I'm still trying to escape it myself."

"There is no escaping it." Her voice was so flat and hopeless it made me study the minor nuances of her face. "I talked to Mikey when I was in that faraway place. I don't know where it was, but I saw him. Saw him for real. He said we needed to switch places and that he lived in the attic of the Mind Mansion."

"Yeah." I choked out, not knowing the best way to respond to the utter truths she threw at me. "That's right."

She chewed on her lip with consternation. "He said he lived there, but that it wasn't his home. That...made sense to me."

I sighed, willing the traitorous tears away to no avail. "He said I had an issue with letting things go. And I do. I..."

"Vonnie, listen to me. Okay?" She gripped me tight. "It's all right. He's in a better place. I just know it."

A pregnant silence hung in the night air that chilled by the passing minute. I hugged her closer to me in spite of the gust of the divisive winds that blew by us.

I opened my mouth to tell her the scary thing my heart wanted, but paused when she blurted, "I think we need time apart!"

My mouth fell open. "W-What?!"

I could see her throat bob as she gulped for the courage to get her through the next speech I dreaded. No, this couldn't be happening. This couldn't be the end before we began.

"Yes. I've been thinking about it as I stared at the lake. I think this is the best option. I don't think you realize how scared I was when you slipped

into that coma. I'd never been that afraid of anything, not even during my sister's sentencing.
I thought I'd die from the fucking heartache. I
thought I could be your peace, but I just cause you
pain."

"No, you don't—"

"Stop it, all right?" She bellowed, her voice ring-
ing out into the night sky and rattling me. But I
held on. Didn't dare release her for fear of floating away and losing her for good like she was
threatening. "I'm the reason you seized up. I'm
the one at fault for putting you in that coma. It's
always me...always me doing the hurting instead
of healing."

"No. No. You don't, Babydoll. I'm the reason for
my own pain. I don't let things go and let love
in. Quit blaming yourself for my own bullshit. It's
me!"

She looked into the sky, as if praying before she
answered. "Either way. I've made up my mind.
This is what's best. What makes sense."

I breathed in deep before revealing this to her.
The scary thing I dreaded would push her away
instead of the opposite I so desperately needed.

"Kimmy. I remember. Everything."

Her anguish morphed into bewilderment as
she drew back to peer into my eyes again. "What?"

"It's true." I said. "I remember everything."

"You mean...?"

"Yes." I finished. "Everything. When we made love at the lake and how good you made me feel. The long talk we had at the lake the first night you moved into town. We'd talked for hours and hours. About your family and my fucked up past. I even remembered the last three months."

She drew in a shaky breath before parting our bodies slightly. "Vonnie, I thought you'd dissociated during all that. Thought I was talking to Mikey all those times...so the last three months when Jeremy banned you from the house and we snuck around—"

"Look at me." I cupped her face, bringing her bouncing eyes to meet mine. "I do. I don't exactly know why I can suddenly recall all these moments, but after Devin came home and asked me to move in with him, it made me think of you. I was suddenly grateful for those treasured memories shared between Mikey and me because it made me realize what was important."

Her cheeks flushed bright red before averting her gaze. Again, she jerked to free herself from my arms, but I denied her.

"Vonnie…" Her voice was small and hopeful. "You remembered all of our time together? Even our kiss before my granny's funeral?"

I kissed her lips lightly. "How can I forget that kiss? Now the memory of it is back, there's no way I'd forget it. I remembered the snorts you made when you laughed at all my jokes, too."

Her throaty laughter broke up the tension between us and fear in my heart. I wanted to share her genuine chuckles, but…I just had to drive the point home. Had to have her understand all the dark recesses of the Mind Mansion and tenderest parts of my stone heart.

"I don't think you understand what you are to me." I breathed.

Kimberly's small smile grew coy as she stared into my eyes. Our lips met in a kiss, so brief, so flickering, it almost felt as if it didn't happen at all. A harsh wind blew by us as Monday's moon shone brightly above our heads, the impact of the gust flushed our bodies close together, her front meeting mine.

"Ooh, s-sorry." She muttered, embarrassed by her actions.

Since we were eye level, it was no problem for me to caress her cheek with my palm.

My sweet Kimmy, I thought lovingly. God she was all I wanted. All I needed. And the only place I ever wanted to be.

I couldn't hide the smile that tugged at my lips. "Babydoll, don't apologize. I knew you just couldn't help yourself from being as close to me as possible. I know it completes you."

Despite the wintry Virginia winds, a flash of heat surged to her pale cheeks as she slapped me playfully on my shoulder.

"You *complete* me with your closeness? Now you're just fishing." She laughed.

I chewed on my lip as I watched her head tilt back with laughter. Gosh, I don't know what was with me tonight, but her every move seemed graceful, her every word I clung to. Perhaps waking up from a near death sleep had its way of making one appreciate a moment.

I chuckled and tightened my arms around her slim frame. "Fishing? But aren't I just sooo cute?"

She smirked. "You're incorrigible."

I smiled devilishly. "And you're my everything."

Her face turned stone serious as she assessed mine. Her arms tightened round my neck as she lowered her lips close to mine. "Don't do this to me."

I frowned slightly, and realized the events of the day and how much I needed her to see I now meant it.

My thick curls blew in the wind as another gust of wind blew straight through my thicker arms, and I allowed all the humor to drain from my next words.

Savoring the delight within her arms, I leaned in close to press my lips to her ear.

"Wherever you're not, my soul is lost." My words were deadpan.

She looked away, and I thought I caught a tear forming in her eyes. My hand shot out to gently grasp her chin, bringing her eyes to meet mine. No way was she running from this.

"You *are* everything." I whispered, falling and feeling myself become captive in her eyes and enraptured by her love. "You are home…"

She nodded. "I know. I know. You're all I ever wanted, Vonnie. I'll do anything to make you feel seen, heard, and loved."

I kissed her, my body burning. "Ditto. I love you, too."

Suddenly, I'm overcome, and the world spins a bit as I grip her tighter to me.

"Baby, you okay?"

"I'm fine. Just a lot of excitement for my first day back with the living."

Her green eyes are shining with concern as she holds me. "Okay. Maybe we should head back to the house. You need your rest."

I push against her, separating our bodies a little. "No. I've done enough resting. Done hiding from my feelings and feeling like I'm not good enough to be beside you."

"You are good enough! I love you, and that makes you better than anything I'd ever imagined for myself." She rushes the heartfelt words out as if I'd slip away. But I won't. And I don't, since I find myself sinking to the grassy field.

This was it. The perfect spot, away from the public eye and by the lake that brought us together.

"What are you doing?" She questioned, as I dropped one wobbly knee to the ground.

I peered up into her worried green eyes, and trusted my gut and love for her to power my next words.

"Kimberly. We've had a rocky road to start, and I appreciate every damn thing about my life now that you're in it. I'm not one for sappy words, but I do know constants and love, two things living on the farm taught me. If you choose me, a long life with me, then I promise to always be your home. Just as you're mine. My forever and always."

"Vonnie!" She exclaims through the sobs, sinking to meet and wrap her arms around me. "Are you asking me what I think you are?"

"Marry me?" I whispered, holding her tight and binding her to my soul.

For always.

EPILOGUE

8 MONTHS LATER

"You cheating scoundrel!" Mamma Dean roared while rising to her feet in fury. In a quick, frightening moment I barely registered coming from my normally-sweet, adopted granny, the game controller flew into the thin flat screen.

My flat screen.

I stood up, too. "Mamma Dean! What the heck was that?"

As if remembering herself, she casts a guilty glance around my old bedroom before saying, "Sorry, Vonnie. I guess I got carried away in all the excitement of the alien game and I didn't realize my own actions."

My eyes were still wide as saucers, but I did little to quell the amused smile that formed on my lips. "Don't worry about it."

"But you gotta admit: that Krimzon is a son of a bitch! Popping up and surprising me like that when my fleet touched down on StinsGar. After all we did to rescue his ass from the Zeldarian prison, too?!" She sucked her teeth, a prominent frown on her face. "I ought to get a refund on this damn game."

The threatening pressure in my gut and chest explodes and I'm doubling over in raucous laughter.

"Mamma Dean." I choke out, barely containing my bladder at this point. "It's only a game. Why you gettin' this worked up over a traitorous alien?"

"It's not funny." She harrumphed like a petulant child instead of the eighty-year-old she was. "I put real effort into that rescue mission, Vonnie. Why didn't you tell me all that was gonna be for nothing? Would've never let you teach me how to play it if I knew that."

"That's sort of the point." I answered, sobering from the laugh attack her tantrum threw me into. "We can play *Weapons from Zeldar 4* whenever you're ready?"

She threw her hands up in exasperation while walking towards the door. "Hell to the no! Cheatin ass game."

I smirked at her. "Really?"

"Yup." She grumbled petulantly.

"Really? You're satisfied with Krimzon ruling over all of Zeldar? After all that hard work you went through to free his traitorous ass?"

"Language." She growled psychosomatically; a considering look on her face. "And...fine! Fire up game four after the pre-reception cookout tonight."

I shook my head at my stubborn old granny, the one who'd always have my heart and gratitude for indulging my gaming habits.

"Yes, ma'am. I'll meet you downstairs in a minute."

"No rush, baby." She answered casually before heading out. "I know y'all got a lot of packin to do before all the guests get here tomorrow for the ceremony."

Shortly after waking up from that strange coma and regaining all my memories (and some of Mikey's, too), Mamma Dean cornered me into teaching her how to play some of my video games. No hardcore online stuff, referring to my virtual gaming fleet usually comprised of *ErnestoCrestOH!*, *Lizardlizardlemons04*, and *NotyourMama_hi5*. Who was I kidding? I'd never needed to be cornered into a gaming sesh, and teaching Mamma Dean the ropes of my most coveted one intensified my love for it. I gazed at the white Food Lion bag across the room that lay intentionally on my empty dresser top. I still hadn't opened Zay's gift from my birthday all those months ago. That was almost a year ago, I summed, as I crossed the room and unsheathed the game inside, *Weapons from Zeldar 4*, which was being sold worldwide by now. Back when my favorite homie picked it up for me, it had been on prerelease and a golden needle to get. I remembered him mentioning the strings he had to pull to get it for me, and I resolved myself to ask him the details when I pulled the game fully from the shopping bag.

Vibrant designs showcased the front cover and provided vivid imagery for the yellow alien aiming his space gun at the viewer. A warm smile spread across my face in anticipation of playing for the first time, finally, since reentering the world of the living. Mamma Dean, Kimmy, and I made it our personal vow and mission to replay games one through three before firing up the highly sought-after *Weapons from Zeldar 4*. Between planning the wedding, my and Kimmy's move, and the weekly Sunday communions, it left us little time to play, but since my fiancée was in town on business, she politely agreed to let Mamma Dean and me finish up the third game.

My heart warmed as the image of my gorgeous ray of sunshine, Kimberly Gresham, popped into my head. We'd been engaged and dating for nearly a year, and every day spent with her taught me something new and brought me closer to her. For instance, she helped me conquer my fear of swimming, considering it was one of her most coveted past times and something I vowed never to do since Mikey's demise. Well, to be totally honest, I wasn't anywhere near out of the woods with my fear of submersion, but my fear dwindled more and more each passing day as we practiced at the lake or rec center in town.

As for that errand she ran in town today? That was all me. I giggle as I recalled pushing my fearful partner out the door this morning. She agreed to reapply to college, and the first step was to meet with the admissions counselor at UVA to discuss her options. A stray tear coursed down her cheek as she stared into her bowl of cheerios this morning at the breakfast table.

"What if they say it's too late for me to go back? Or that my grades aren't good enough to transfer?" She whispered brokenly.

I grabbed hold of her chin, forcing our eyes to rendezvous. "Hey, Babydoll, that won't happen. Come on, you told me you had nearly perfect scores in your classes at RowanU?"

"I did. Sort of. There was this one class I withdrew from in the middle of the semester, and last I checked, the grade wasn't so good since I had to leave college so suddenly. My grades suffered..."

"You got this, babe. Besides, you're all muscle with the smarts and brave as hell. I admire that about you."

Her cheeks warmed. "Thanks, my love. I'll try to suck this up and go to that appointment today. You're right. I got this!"

"Damn, right!" I hackled. "Kimberly Gresham-Carlson for the win, baby!"

"Yessss!" Happy tears pricked her eyes as we shimmied together in that weird but cute way whenever we got excited. I frowned at her when she froze up, however. "Babe, would you consider going to school?"

The question took me aback so severely I only stared at her.

She adjusted before adding, "I think it'll be good for you; you know? Maybe take a few night classes to start until you get the hang of it."

School and my future were two of those things that settled into the gray area of my life. I never got along with strangers and had such severe social anxiety I'd opted to skip my high school graduation altogether. My diploma arrived in the mail about a month after the ceremony I missed.

I shook my head. "Nope. I'm good on that."

"You mean to tell me you're fine with working on the farm for the rest of your life? Don't you have dreams? Ambitions?"

I choked down the emotion enough to respond to her through gritted teeth. "Please drop this, okay? Let's focus on you today. And your achievements. This is a big day for you, babe. The first step towards your dream."

"But what about your dreams?" She shot back in gentle rapid fire. "UVA has an excellent Graphic Design program."

Again, I allowed my eyes to do the answering like in my voiceless days. A few moments passed before she resigned, however.

"Just give it some thought, okay? That's all I ask."

I gave a halfhearted nod before she left for her appointment. I hated telling her how content I was staying on the farm with my patchwork family. Even though we were moving in a couple of days into our own house, it wouldn't be far, since it was a vacant cabin left behind by a former resident farmhand. The cozy little one bedroom was perfect for us and our new beginning, but also on the farm. I had no desire to leave the haven I created with her here, and a part of me was hurt that she'd suggested it.

Shaking the memory away, I slid the game back into the bag to consider later when a white piece of paper fell from it.

My eyes bugged as I examined the typewriter font etched on the rectangular piece of paper. A receipt. Not only did the exorbitant price tag on this game shock me to the core, but so did the name preceding it at the top of the page.

Shamel M.

Did I read that right? The final four digits of a credit card were visible under the name I didn't recognize, and I was assailed with a strange mixture of confusion and anger. Just what, and who, was this person? Did Zay steal this from some innocent guy in town? Couldn't be, I figured, laughing at the image of Zay committing any sort of crime since all he'd ever been was playful and lazy as hell in the five years I'd known him. But I couldn't help considering the outrageous theft notion: If so, why go to the trouble? All for me?

So many questions lingered in my mind that I didn't notice the man at the door.

Devin popped his head inside my nearly empty room. "Yo, Von. You bout ready?"

"Jesus!" I yelped while clutching a hand to my chest. "Don't sneak up on me like that, Dev. Want me to die on my wedding day?"

The smile I expect from him doesn't come, as he flashes me that serious frown I'd become all too accustomed to whenever I'd do something wrong from that past life in DC.

"Vonnie don't joke like that. Of course, I don't want that."

I shoved the note in my back pocket before raising my hands in defeat. "Only a joke. Remember what that is? A joke? Haha?"

A faint smile shadows his lips. "Oh, yeah, right. Sorry. I still get a little freaked out when you make morbid jokes like that. Especially since your coma. My bad, Von."

I crossed the room towards him and threw reassuring arms around my brother. "No biggie. I get it."

"Besides," he started, a light rumble rocked his chest that I instantly recognized as laughter. "Your wedding day is tomorrow. Not today. So don't go making dying jokes with the wrong date."

"Noted." I cupped my sides from the restrained laughter before asking, "what's up?"

"Malik is here to cut your hair like he promised. He's waiting for you in the basement. Got the chair all set up for you and everything."

"Shit, I forgot about that." I breathed guilty before jetting down the hall. "Thanks for the reminder!"

"No sweat," he provided before jogging in the direction of the living room once we got downstairs. "I'll be right back, though."

"Where are you going? Is Rome all right?" I asked, concern heating my face from the prospect of my precious nephew being anything less than okay.

He waved a dismissive hand. "Lil man is good. Shay got him until she goes to work tonight. Plus, I'm meeting up with Zay and Bone for some errands."

I lifted inquisitive brows at the former. "Shay, huh? So, you guys are a 'thing' again?"

"Von," he whined, pausing. "Don't start this with me. Yes, me and Shay are talking. That's all you need to know. All right?"

"Not all right!" I hissed excitedly as I ran over to him. "This is major news."

"You mean, juicy gossip?"

"No!" I lied emphatically, knowing damn well this news would make just the thing for Kimmy and I to gossip about later. "Really, this is a huge development. Shay wanted nothing to do with your ass when you came back. Wouldn't even come over for Mamma Dean's Sunday brunches."

He winced. "I know. I know. I did her dirty. But I've been…trying with her. Trying to show her instead of telling her with my words that I'm a dumbass for leaving her high-and-dry for five years. A lot of stuff went down for both of us while we were apart."

I want to keep pressing him, lord knows I did, but the question dies in my throat as I gaze upon his tormented frown. It's like he's reliving five years of hell in a matter of five seconds.

"Stay strong, Dev." I whispered with frail hope as I slapped his shoulder. "I don't know all of what happened between you guys, especially since Zay, Shay, nor you will let me in on it like I'm still a child but listen. Just listen to her. You might be surprised."

He nodded, savoring the flavor of my words as I spoke with that concentrated look Rome carbon copied from him. "Okay. I think I will. I know just what to do. Thanks, Von."

"Anytime, bro," I trilled before hugging him tight and heading towards my long-awaited hair appointment.

"Here comes the bride." Malik sings when I make it to the basement door panting.

The entire room, which is normally reserved for family sized guests considering it had a bathroom attachment, is lit up like a Christmas tree. I mean it. There are so many lights on I forget the pain in my lungs from running down here for a second as I creep down the steps.

Bone Thugs N Harmony's "Thuggish, Ruggish, Bone," is playing on the speaker, but it's so low I don't hear it until I'm all the way inside. Or, rather, down under.

"Malik, I'm sorry I'm late!" I lament as I approach the tall onyx skinned man. Instead of his usual beater and shorts, he's fully robed in barber attire: a tan smock covers his chest and arms along with khaki style pants. Since getting his barber gig in the city, I'd never seen him out of his usual setting of homeboy, so this was...refreshing. No, odd, was more like it, as I sank into the lone chair in the middle of the room.

"It's all good, lil Von." He chants easily, rocking back and forth to the low music. "Remember, you're doing me the honor of extra practice."

I smiled as he gathered my thick curls in his hands. "Well, okay then. We're square. And I appreciate you for doing this at such an odd hour. I wanted to make sure this was done before Kimmy gets back from her appointment."

He's already snipping away by the time he asks, "You keeping this a secret?"

"Not really...just want this to be my choice, you know? It's my hair and I'll do with it what I want. I never really liked...all of this anyways."

He snorts. "On some female empowerment shit. I feel that. But your fiancée might not like you doing it behind her back."

"I'm not hiding it!" I growled, my anger rising. "It's just my prerogative. My hair. My call."

"Okay." He quips, as if there's thousands more he wants to say but allows the answering silence to fester the awkwardness.

The rest of the session flies by with several other rap classics playing in the background. A cool gush of wind breezes by and I feel it on my scalp.

"Voila." He mutters appreciatively before handing me a mirror. "Check my handiwork."

"Malik..." I breathed in utter...satisfaction. Delight might be the best word for the warm tingles flowing over me as I gaze at the short fade. My former luscious locks Mamma Dean coveted dearly to her heart were now a thing of the past, as I glanced at the pile of curls on the floor. Hair was everywhere, on me, Malik, and all over the floor, but it barely resonated against the thudding of my heart. I felt more like myself than I ever did, a sense of sheer completeness settling over me, same as when I whipped out a video game. This was me. All me. A new me, with a bright future and home.

"You don't like it? Fuck, my bad Vonnie. I'll—" I interrupted his doubtful apologies by standing and throwing my arms around him. He returns the hug, and his rich laughter shakes me to my core. "I guess I did a good job."

"Oh yeah." I mewled, pulling away from him with a smile.

A deep rose colored his dark cheeks as he averted a sheepish gaze. "Glad I can make you smile. Anytime, for real. You my home girl."

"Solid," I agreed, exchanging convivial fist bumps. "I appreciate you, but I do need to go help Mamma Dean prepare for the cookout tonight. You know all them guests are coming."

"Wait!" He barked, making me flinch from fright. He cleared his throat and tried again. "My bad, um, you want to play some cards or something?"

I frowned. "Uh, no. I gotta go."

"No!" He urged with a hand on my arm now. "Stay for a minute. Down here. With me. Um, we can talk some more, maybe?"

"What?"

"What video games you been playing lately?" His tone got nervous, which made me nervous from the weird behavior. Malik normally took life too seriously, but this was totally out of character and freaking me out.

I yanked my arm away to no avail. "Malik, you know what games I play, get off me. You gettin a little too close."

His eyes alternate between me and the door, but he doesn't let go.

Infuriated, I punched his exposed right arm with my free hand.

"Ah, shit! Ouch!" He bellowed while I twisted out of his hold. Fear rose inside of me as I ran for the steps. I had to borrow Mikey's term, since I was triggered all over as I ascended the basement steps with Malik hot on my heels.

Just as I readied myself to kick his teeth in, the door opened.

There stood to my shock, Xavier, Devin, and Bone at the threshold. Each held a pack of beers and sneaky grins on their faces.

"What is this?" I demanded, winded and furious. "What's going on?"

Zay kept his smile devilish as he answered. "Everybody's left the house and Mamma Dean agreed we could kick it for a couple of hours before the cookout."

"This is your bachelor party, *Chica*." Bone inserted before tumbling passed me down the stairs. "Time to party up!"

"No! I don't want this, you guys." I groaned, suddenly understanding that random errand of Devin's from earlier and Malik's unusual caginess to keep me from leaving the basement.

"Oh, but you do." Zay threw his free arm around my shoulders before guiding me back downstairs.

"I do not." I grunted, suddenly tired from the idea of drinking and smoking.

"Do, too." Zay teased.

In a split second, I turned in his arm and ran for the door. Well, I attempted to run, since Devin's lingering presence behind us stops me dead in my tracks.

"Sorry, sis." He mumbles apologetically. "I told him this wasn't your vibe, but he insisted you'd wanted to party up before the wedding."

Warmth floods me at Devin's keen knowledge of me even after all these years. "Thanks, bro. Now why can't *they* see reason?"

He shrugged, "They don't listen. I told them you only liked gaming in your room all day. That you don't do much hanging out with the people in real life and preferred your gamer friends. I'll tell them this was a waste of time if—"

"Hold up." I stopped him with an affronted glare and raised hand. "I prefer my gamer friends? A waste of time?"

"Uh, yeah."

"Uh, no!" I countered, apoplectic. "Just who do y'all think I am? Some boring stick in the mud that can't have fun?"

The room grew eerily silent, and I growled at their quiet consensus as I stared at them.

"You not a stick in the mud, Von!" Bone choked between puffs off his blunt. "You just...real particular about your time. That's it."

"Oh, y'all think I can't hang?" I replied as a rise to the challenge stirring in the room.

"Can you?" Zay asked.

Turns out, I sure could. Three hours ticked by in a flurry of fat joints and Hennessey. Neither me nor Devin take sips of the liquor being passed, but wc all take shared hits from the sweet Mary Jane working the room. There's a sofa and a king-sized bed down here, and I'm only vaguely aware of Zay sitting to my right and Devin half asleep and slumped over to my left. Bone and Malik are engaged in a typical argument, but it's not so heated due to the heavy indica they finished smoking.

"Pass that shit, Von." Zay requests lazily, and I do. "You look tired."

I chuckled. "Nah. Not tired. Just a little floaty right now."

"Floaty..." he sings in a contented whisper. "Floaty like a goatee, I am a coyote..."

I never stopped chuckling, but say, "What the fuck are you rapping about, man?"

He swiped a hand over his face. "I don't fucking know. I'm so faded and dumb right now."

I steal the joint before chanting, "Dumb. Dumb. I'm dumb, you're dumber."

"Aye!" He cackles before catching on. "If you're fun, I'm funner!"

"It's hot-ter than summer!" I added while swaying to the unheard beat in my head. The chuckle-then-verse I expected from Zay doesn't come and when I glance at him he's staring hauntedly into the wall. "You good?" I questioned, worry replacing the giddy convivial vibes.

"Nah." He said.

"Why?"

"Because."

"Because what?"

"Because of Sommer."

"Summer?" I asked, a giggle creeping its way into my chest again at another one of his intoxicated ramblings. "What about summer?"

"Do you remember New Jersey?" His question was rapid fire at me.

"What? When?"

He sucked in his teeth. "Fuck, of course you wouldn't remember. You were so little. Both of y'all."

"Both?"

"Yeah. You and Michael. Y'all was so little when you'd come and visit us in the PJ's." A reminiscent smile curled his face as he leaned back against the sofa. He looked kind of how I felt, floaty amidst the smoke clouds in the air. "Damn I miss those days. I miss my mom, too."

An eerie fright settled somewhere in my chest, slowing my heart a bit as I listened to his inebriated uttering. He's not making any sense, I figured, and I almost dismiss him until his next words freeze me in place.

"Sommer is my mom's name. She's still in Camden. She still calls, but I don't let Shay know. She'd be so pissed off."

He sounds like he's drifting away on a cloud and unaware anyone was in the same room.

"Sommer...?" I uttered, my mind reeling in efforts to remember why that name sounded so familiar. Why that information seemed so spot on for a split second and slipping away in the next.

Find Sommer. Find Sommer. Quincy's ghost's words hit me like a sack of bricks all of a sudden.

Surely, this couldn't be...

I open my eyes wide before demanding. "Where did you get that game, Zay?"

"What...game?" He slurs.

I punched his arm, but he doesn't budge as he sinks deeper into the couch. I know he's about to join Devin in the realm of dreamland, so I rush to blurt the question out.

"*Weapons from Zeldar*...come on, I know you remember. My birthday gift."

"Hmmm..." He sings sleepily while twisting in his seat. "That alien shit?"

"Yeah!" I nodded eagerly, already feeling the post-high paranoia sinking in. "Did you steal it from some guy, fuck, what was his name? Right! Um, Shamel?"

Was this the reason Quincy urged me to 'play the game?' His warning lingers like a distant bomb in my mind as I await my homie's response.

"Game was so expensive. Had to dig into my No Touch stash to buy it. Shay says I got to let Devin be your brother and not overstep. I told her, 'damn it Shay, I'm her brother, too.'"

Now that I laugh at, feeling relieved he's back to kidding around. "Sure, you are."

"I am." He visibly bristles with annoyance. "I'm really your big brother, Vonnie. I can spoil you as much as I want, too. Shay don't know what she talkin 'bout."

"Sure, you are." I repeat, teasing him. "Just like you're magically this 'Shamel M' guy from that game receipt, too."

He sits up just then, turns, and extends a rough hand to me. His eyes are completely lucid when he speaks again.

"Name's Shamel Masters. Nice to finally meet you for real, VonVon."

I'm not quite sure when I fell asleep, but my lids are as heavy as dumbbells as I attempt to lift them to see the world and reason. I was on a couch, seemingly alone, as I scanned through the dark room to see...well, darkness. If I squint my eyes, I can make out the outlines of vacant furniture, and I'm aware of Bone, Malik, Devin, and Zay's absence. Where'd everyone go? Did that surprise bachelor party even happen in reality or another figment of Mind Mansion illusion?

The previous events are sort of fuzzy as I struggle to recall them while standing. My entire body is heavy, and it becomes a chore to pull it up the stairs and into the kitchen. Which is empty, but loud music from the front yard blares through the house.

Shit, I swear as I gaze at the crowd of church, farm, and family members communing and Cha-Cha Sliding around the grill. I completely forgot about that pre-reception cookout.

Disoriented, I decide to search for my love and anchor through the foggy uncertainty I awakened to. Kimmy should have returned hours ago from that counselor appointment in town, and I'm frantically weaving through the crowds of "hey, Von!" and "how you doin' child!" to seek out the love of my life. Among the sea of melanin, her fiery red hair sticks out sorely a few feet away.

My heartbeat eases as I witness her.

I find her in the center of old women I recognize as Mary-Mable Jackson and Lucinda Hinton, Malik's maternal grandmother who raised him and his six younger sisters. These ladies make up the better part of Mamma Dean and Aunt Stevie's best gals crew, and they'd been by nearly every day since Aunt Stevie's passing to check on my sweet granny.

Kimmy's holding a giggly infant in her arms who I know as my chunky nephew Romelo.

"Kimmy girl," Lucinda, whom everyone calls Ms. Cindy, addresses my fiancée with raised brows and I can feel the lecture coming. "You look good with that baby on your hip."

She grins sheepishly before tucking back a stray curl. "Thanks, Ms. Cindy."

Ms. Cindy grins slyly. "This farm is gonna need some more chil'un round here. You and your wife talk about how y'all gonna give us some?"

Mary-Mable gave her best friend a playful but ineffectual swat. "Now, Cindy! You know you ain't supposed to be askin her all that."

"But, it's true!" Ms. Cindy exclaimed. "Rome needs some kids around his age he can play with soon as he get big enough. My grands are all grown up and I gots no cheeks to pinch or babies to spoil."

I waited as the brief silence eclipsed the air between them for Kimmy's response. Children were a sore topic for me since I received my diagnosis several years prior. Pelvic Inflammatory Disease, the kind doctor called the insipid disease that ravaged my reproductive organs. Kimmy and I never did discuss our stances on children and if we wanted to reproduce, but curiosity and pain flared in my heart as I awaited her answer to the prying old crows.

"Well," Kimmy began. "Rome here should be all the baby you need for a while."

"Y'all don't want kids?" Mary-Mable chirped suspiciously. "And how would all that work anyway?"

Kimmy rears back, and I can't see her face since I'm several bodies behind her in the crowd, but I hear her retort, loud and clear. "How does what work?"

"You know." Mary-Mable added. "Babies. Between girl and girl?"

"Mary-Mable, behave yourself—"

"I got this." Kimmy interjected Ms. Cindy's ineffectual warning with a raise of her free hand.

"Listen, what my wife and I do with our bodies is our business. We might have kids, we might not—either way, the direction we take our family is decided by us. And no one else."

Ms. Cindy chimed in. "Kimmy, we was just curious—"

"No!" She replies, cold as stone. "You're a part of the problem, you know. Would you ask a heterosexual couple questions like this? Are you not aware of how ignorant and old-world you sound in this day and age? So, respectfully, fuck off."

My, as well as the two bitter crows', jaw dropped in sync. However, pure pride and love weakened my jaw muscles and strengthened my admiration for her. I'm so overcome with emotion and the need to protect her; I find myself cutting through the crowd to reach her.

"Hi, Vonnie." Ms. Cindy greets with the fakest smile on her face. "We was just having a little girl talk with your girl here. Interesting stuff."

"You mean, *woman*. We're grown Ms. Cindy, and she's my fiancée. So, you'll show her some respect, or kindly leave." I wrapped an arm around her waist and pulled her to my side.

A smug grin crested Kimmy's beautiful face, however, until she finally got a good look at me.

"Your hair?" She breathes in abject astonishment as she assesses me with hard green eyes.

I grimace as the memory of what I'd done floats back to me. The haircut I meant to discuss with her in private upon her arrival after that counseling appointment.

Mary-Mable makes a face as she glares at our conjoined bodies. "Just like Hattie and Stevie with that lesbo foolishness."

"What you say?" I barked. A fury so hot and powerful shot through my being, and I'm all of a sudden lunging for her.

Kimmy holds me back and Rome's cries recenter me as my mind wrestles for control.

"Babe, stop. Not worth it, okay? Just forget them."

Mary-Mable must be nearing that age where any and all sense of self-preservation disappears, since she continues. "Hattie and Stevie was always makin' eyes at each other when they got together. Just sickening. Even at church they'd sit side by side like husband and wife. Just turns my insides."

I struggle for control, I do, but the embers of hate rekindle as I close the gap between us to glower into her wrinkled eyes.

"You stay away from this house, you hear me? You bitter old bitches have been nothing but toxic to my sweet grandmother. Where were you, her supposed best friends, after Aunt Stevie died? Your so-called visits don't ever involve you moving past the mailboxes to say 'hi.' Even now, you're only here to gossip and talk shit. I'm so ashamed of you. Both of you!"

Ms. Cindy's eyes are downcast and regretful, but Mary-Mable's indignance is obvious as she tuts three times and hobbles away, pulling an apologetic Ms. Cindy with her.

"Sorry." Ms. Cindy mouths before retreating and leaving us alone.

"Babe, that was *so* boss." Kimmy preens before biting into her hotdog. We now occupied a picnic table towards the very back of the field where the party gathered. Kimmy scarfed the hotdog as I held on to a giggly Romelo. "You owned that entire confrontation. I'm proud of you."

"Don't think I didn't hear you." I say, "told them to fuck off and everything. My fiancée's got balls."

"Hell, yeah." She slides me a sly smile before leaning over. Our kiss is brief and gentle but heats me all over in the best way possible after we part. "Now, tell me, why did you shave your hair?"

Damn it, I swore inwardly, praying the confrontation distracted her from my new do.

I cleared my throat. "You like it?"

Her jaw works a moment as she studies my close shave. "It...it's fitting. You look like you."

Hope filled my heart. "Really? So, you like it?"

She nods, smiling. "Yeah, babe! Besides, how angry could I be with that design in your head?"

"Design?"

"Yeah." She says. "The design shaved into the back."

I only stare at her.

"I assume you didn't know about that."

"Uh, no!"

"Well, it's a date: 08-08. August 8th. Our wedding day, right?"

A warm feeling spreads in my chest at the sweet gesture and surprise design Malik must have carved into my shave.

But I find myself asking her a question that's been plaguing me since finding her out here.

"Where have you been? Wasn't your counseling appointment hours ago?"

"I went to Shay's house. She called me to ask for some advice...and I went over. She was concerned about Zay's gambling addiction and wanted some advice on how to discuss it with him." She mumbles.

"She asked you about it?"

"Yeah, I mean, I can relate after all. We both have stubborn, self-destructive younger brothers. She gave me some advice on how to connect with Jeremy, too, since he moved out to live with our old stepdad Gavin back in East Orange. He barely returns any of my phone calls since he left seven months ago."

"He'll come around, babe." I assure her. "You can't control his actions or what he approves of."

"I know. I don't need his approval, but he's my little brother. I love him and hate that he doesn't want anything to do with me because of my choice to marry the love of my life, you know?" Her face falls with the words.

"News flash boo: I ain't going anywhere. So, Jeremy will come around if he loves and supports you the way you do him."

"My number one fan, huh?"

"Always and forever."

"Gosh, you're amazing."

"As are you." A foul smell hovers in the air and I notice Rome squirm and thrash unhappily in my arms.

"But not this stinky diaper. Please excuse me while I go change this cute baby!"

I hand her the baby while holding my breath. "Just come back soon, babe. There's more I wanna talk about."

"Oh, I'll be back. I need more Vonnie time anyways. Felt like I haven't seen you in forever." She tossed me a flirtatious wink as she balanced the fussy poop machine on her hip.

I laugh good naturedly, understanding her perfectly since the hole in my heart widened a bit since we'd been apart these few hours. We were basically obsessed with each other in the best way, and I can't resist the humongous smile on my face as I watch her float between the crowd towards the house.

"Yo, Von. You got a minute to talk?"

All merriment and good vibes dissipate instantly at the sound of his voice. Of that question. Glancing in its direction, I notice Zay, Malik, and Bone standing about a foot from me. While close, their bodies were swallowed by the night's darkness. Zay stepped forward though.

"What the fuck do you want? And where have you been?" I spat.

He sighed, looking every bit as exhausted as I felt even though I'd just woken up. "Let me just explain. I had a dream I told you some information about me that...just ain't true."

"Oh, you mean the dream in which you told me you were my brother? That you met me and Mikey?"

"Fuck, it really wasn't a dream. I'm sorry, Von. I made it all up, okay? I was high and had a little bit to drink. I wasn't myself, and I apologize for ruining your bachelor party. Let me make it up, okay?"

"Is it...is it true, Zay?" I fight to keep the anger in my tone, but it falters as I do when the tears form. "How, no, *why* are you here? After all this time? If you really are my brother...then did you know this entire time? After five years?"

He nods, a tortuous movement while staring into my watery eyes. "I had my reasons, though. Trust me. I didn't mean for you to find out this way. I promise I didn't mean to hurt you, baby girl. I love you."

"This isn't love. A loving brother wouldn't trick his sister for five years into thinking she was all alone in this world. You could have told me, Zay. Shamel. Whoever you are!"

"It's Shamel." He answers feebly. "Xavier is my middle name. Rose is my mom's last name. Fuck, please don't write me off, VonVon! I did all of this for you."

I just shook my head at his repeated use of that new but vaguely familiar name. "Did Shay know, too?"

"Yes. But it's not her fault. It's all on me. I made her promise not to tell when we followed y'all to Richmond."

"Followed? So that's it. You really are a monster..."

He bends to his knees to meet me at eye level. He fumbles in his Jean pockets for a second before retrieving a square paper. "I wanna give you this."

"What is...?" My words fade as I study the worn paper that's not a paper at all. It's a photograph. Of a dark-skinned skinny boy, of maybe eight or nine, with two toddlers on his lap. All three wear huge smiles and the maybe-eight-year-old encourages the boy toddler in his lap to look at the camera. The little girl, with my face, has orange mush around her mouth but she smiles. They all look identical, and it makes me stare at the now twenty something year old man before with renewed focus and confusion.

"That's us. You, me, and Mike. My Big Mike and VonVon. Y'all were so little, and you were so pissed I took your Cheese Twists away before Shay took that pic."

"We look...just alike. That's me and Mikey? How did you..." I'm hyperventilating from the pain and shock of his reminiscing. But another emotion wells up in me that makes me more nauseated than the pain: Stupid. That about summed up the rush of futility and anger swirled together like a stupidity tornado crashing my common sense. How could I not have realized this sooner? The Master's family had one distinct trait, our pointed noses and wide eyes, and Zay could have been my father's twin since he owned every aspect of Masters genes.

He reaches out to steady me as I nearly faint. "Hey, calm down. I'll explain everything, I promise. I had planned to do it after the wedding, but..."

"You're really Quincy's son?" My voice is hollow.

He nods, a bitter sneer twisting his face. "Unfortunately. He wasn't much of a dad though."

"What happened to him, then? Our father?" I uttered faintly.

He averted his eyes. "He's dead."

"I know! But what happened?!"

He shook his head. "No. I'm not going into that with you."

"Talk. Now. Or you can all leave." I yank his shirt forward to force his eyes to meet mine.

To my shock, Zay doesn't even fight me. Just casts me a look so filled with guilt it makes me shiver.

"He told us everything, Von." Bone interjected, the forever mediator. "Just give your big bro a chance to hear him out. He's been through a lot to get here."

"Please, Vonnie. We still your homies." Malik adds apologetically.

"Leave me alone. All of you! Go away!"

Zay reaches out for me, but I slap him senseless before I can stop myself. There was so much anger bubbling inside of me from the night's events that I unleashed it all on my supposed "brother's" face.

"I don't want to see your fucking face tomorrow, Zay. Are we clear?" I thundered, forcing him to meet my eyes and understand that I meant every word.

I was done with him.

He nodded again, his face contorted into a grimace that mimics a glare as he and the guys trail off. I'm almost sure he grumbles, "I'll fix this," before a sound catches my attention. Or, rather, Mamma Dean is clearing her throat to make her presence politely known after that altercation with Zay. Or Shamel. Or whoever the fuck he was.

Because no way was I accepting him as my blood after this.

"Yvonne, not sure if you heard earlier, but this here is Patrice. You remember her?" Mamma Dean preened with the biggest smile on her face. Well, until some of the bonfire lights illuminated us enough for her to catch a glimpse of my buzz-cut. I watch her eyes saucer for a moment before she sobers with a pretty fake smile.

"Not sure I remember. Sorry."

I recognize her instantly, though I lie through my teeth after studying the interracial couple before me.

Mamma Dean sucks her teeth admonishingly before replying, "Yvonne, you're telling me you don't remember, Patrice? I seem to recall reading something about a girl named Trice in your diary a couple weeks back. She matches the description of the girl you wrote about."

A diary? Eerie realization settles into my bones as I recognize her reference to Mikey's journal.

"Mamma Dean! What did I tell you about going through my things?"

"Why don't y'all have a little talk? Get reacquainted?"

I crossed my arms. "I told you, old woman. I don't know her!"

"What's going on?" The voice of an angel cuts in, her green eyes assessing the situation with a wary protectiveness. It's Kimmy, holding Rome in her arms, and the sight of her brings a wave of calm to my stormy soul. I want to cuss, to hurt someone or something, but I know this has nothing to do with Trice or Devin's former friend, Kale. This has everything to do with my undealt feelings toward losing Mikey's sunlit presence in my mind and gaining Zay's conniving one in my life. What was a girl to do with these unwashed emotions?

"It's nothing, babe. Mamma Dean just being Mamma Dean." I tell her, to ease that worried look she got that drove me crazy with guilt.

I'm barely present as we all sit down at the table. Kimmy and Trice rattle on about something I'm not giving any attention to as my mind reels from...well, everything. What was Zay's motive in all this? And why was he lying to me all this time? I'm so livid I could spit, but something Trice murmurs snaps my attention to her and triggers all that anger.

"I didn't ask you to be a part of it!" I snarl at her previous declaration of being 'so happy to be a part of our special day.' "What's your agenda, huh?"

She pops her neck at me. "Excuse me?"

"You hear me." I bark, pinning evil eyes on her. "What's your deal? Here to fuck with my brother's head again?"

"Vonnie!" Kimmy warns, and I'm aware I'm going off the deep end and over a cliff as my hands start trembling. But this seed of hate in me...it just won't let go. After being kept in the dark for so long about my father's death and Zay's grand lie, the seed of hate begins to burst forth, morphing into a beautiful agent of destruction.

Trice, for all intents and purposes, did fuck with Devin's head all those years ago when they dated, and I never really got all the details of their relationship, but I'm sure it's a long story. A long story that brings me a new thought.

"You know, I think she's the reason he enlisted." I told Kimmy, thinking of the way Devin's eyes would gleam sullenly whenever I asked about his reasons for enlisting. He'd only ever looked like that when he spoke about Patrice Newbern. The girl he, for some reason, could never fully shake.

Trice cleared her throat before a pained expression marred her face. "I see something sparked your memory. Yvonne, honey, you don't know what you're talking about. Please—"

"You need to leave!" I growl with a menacing affect as I cross my arms. I didn't want the DC reminders of my awful past. Didn't want to deal with the pity in Trice's eyes as she studied me, the once frail little girl turned mentally ill young adult. She, and whoever else she arrived here with, needed to go.

Kimmy's voice reaches me, penetrates the hate fog I'm too enveloped in as I glare at Trice. "Baby, your center. Find your center, remember?"

Her words bring calm to my storm. Light to my dark, and redemption for all the shame. So much fucking shame.

"Find my center." I mutter on a shaky breath. "Find the beacon. The center is home."

The sky crackles with the promise of a treacherous rainstorm I remembered learning about from the news this morning. When things were simple. This morning I woke up so happy and prepared to begin this wedding and journey with my beautiful bride. But now? Again, only hot shame and frustration surged through my being.

"Vonnie?" I hear my brother call from the same darkness that enshrouded Zay a few minutes ago. "What's all this yelling about? Is Zay still here?"

I open my mouth to tell him, like the dutiful little sister in me normally defaults to doing whenever he asks me a question, but I freeze. My voice gets trapped in my throat like it used to when I was little, and I'm in the basement again. My eyes shut and screams tormenting my innocence and ears.

In a flash, I run away from there. I'm running, same as I did when Lucy the Evil bargained me for that favor during that last day of my innocence. Except, this time, there's no concrete for me to trip over as I make the short jog through the grass to the one place that's allowed me to breathe since coming to live on the farm.

The lake.

The moonlight dances across the murky waters as I inhale deep to cherish it all.

Peace. This was peace. A quiet away from the storm of my life and mind, but my heart is still a frenzy. Racing faster than I'm able to handle as I dip a tentative toe into the cool water. Warm wind blows by me, almost as if the warm caress of encouragement I need to jump in. But I don't jump in; instead, I ease myself slowly into the placid waters amidst the storm brewing in sky and in my heart.

I just wanted it to stop. I wanted the mansion in my head to just stop consuming me and swallowing my memories as they did my baby brother. The thought of him, of Mikey, makes me want to sink into the deep end, but I take a deep breath when the water reaches my shoulders.

Kimmy taught me how to float, and I rather enjoyed the sensation of buoyantly tracking across the calm waters. Though submerging myself completely in water was triggering, I did the unthinkable and plunged my head in. Clear my mind and let my body become light as air, was the advice my almost-wife gave me several days after waking from the against-the odds coma a few months back. My eyes are shut, and I truly try to do as she instructed, but images of Zay's crestfallen face as he told me the truth of his existence as well as the look on Trice's face while I berated her unfairly makes me feel anything but light. I'm struggling to clear my mind to grasp onto the tranquility that comes with floating, but I can't. My chest is heavy from holding my breath too long, and I give way to full blown panic as I thrash around in the too deep waters.

The water is cool and omnipresent: invading every hole in my body and making breathing impossible.

Right before delirium kicks in, strong hands pull me from the water.

"Yvonne! Babe, it's me. Oh my gosh, please be breathing." Kimmy's flustered voice reaches me as I choke on the liquid in my lungs.

I'm aware that she's laid me on the grass and that I'm now in her arms. It's fully raining now, no, storming as she takes my chin in her hands to guide my eyes to hers.

"What was that? Did Trice offend you or something?"

I shook my head, sputtering. "No. Not Trice."

"Then who? Then what? What made you run off and dive into the lake? *You. Can't. Swim.* Why do this?" She's screeching at this point, and I'm suddenly cognizant of the anger and concern in her tone.

"Babe!" I call to her over the thunder. "I'm okay. Stop worrying. I was trying to float in the lake, that's it."

"That's it?" She mimicked, skeptic and furious. "This conversation isn't over, Yvonne Carlson."

"You've got nothing to worry about babe." I assured her in bed several minutes later. We made it to the room, dried off, and collapsed into an exhausted heap once we made it to my old bedroom. "I'm fine."

Her arms encircled me under the covers. "I don't believe that."

"But I am!" I reiterate pointedly, signaling my level of done with the mental check in.

"But you're lying. Again. We're getting married tomorrow, and you still feel like you can't trust me with the truth? If that's the case, then what's all this for?"

I don't answer her. Don't even look at her as she continues her rant.

She leans her forehead against mine. "I see you, Vonnie. Always remember that. It's only because I see you for who you really are that I'm being hard on you. You gotta let me in. Because what that looked like to me when I found you in that lake—"

"Okay. Okay." I hiss, my chest hurting from the truth in her words. But I'm also tired of holding on to all of this burden alone. I take a deep breath before letting her all the way inside the Mind Mansion of information.

"Zay is my brother." I whisper.

She pulls back to stare at me, frowning. "Yeah, you guys are close. Did something happen with him?"

I nodded.

"What?"

I sighed. "Zay is my biological brother. I know it sounds really crazy and hard to believe but it's the truth. He showed me a picture of the three of us...and I can't understand why he'd tell me this after all this time. Or why he even moved here, fooling me this entire time by being my friend when he was really just a stalker."

Kimmy sits up. "Maybe he had his reasons, babe."

I sit up beside her to toss a confused expression her way. "What? What could possibly constitute his reason for following us here five years ago and living on the farm under an alias? That's insane! And I want nothing to do with him. He's dead to me, as far as I'm concerned."

A nervous expression takes hold of her precious round face, and I frown at her chewing on her bottom lip.

"You okay?" I say, a little astounded by how well she was receiving this life shattering news.

Her wince makes my heart stutter before she says. "There's something you should know."

"You almost ready?"

Devin, who's dressed in military regalia, asks as he pokes his head inside my room. Today is the day I'd dreamt and hoped for, but never believed could ever be meant for me: My wedding day.

Despite the storm that bathed the farm in a furious downpour, the sun is shining as if there'd been no record of yesterday. Perhaps, this was a metaphor for my bright future with Kimmy in spite of the dark days before her, but the news she gave me last night...makes me hesitate.

She'd harbored that secret for so long, and I'm not sure if my usual blind trust in her could ever restore itself after what she told me last night. So many secrets, lies, and deception, I think sadly as I stare at the solid gray band on my right ring finger.

We'd taken the non-traditional route for our wedding by wearing the rings we chose in our favorite colors before the ceremony. Hers a mahogany band that gleams under the sun, a "forever reminder of my beautiful brown eyes," she insisted on wearing on her finger. And mine, a charcoal gray that symbolized the balance and stabilizing effect Kimmy brought me. Gray was also Devin's favorite color, which made me smile to incorporate a piece of the man who'd protected me all these years.

Was this wedding the greatest chapter of my story, or the beginning of a more tragic one?

"I'm almost ready." I tell him absently while staring into the body length mirror.

The white, fitted, pants suit creates a striking contrast against my mocha skin. My clean cut enhances my sharp features from the Masters genes. I marvel at the pointed nose I got from my father, and the round cheeks from Lucy's.

No, not Lucy, I correct myself, but Helen Cooper's round cheeks and wide smile I'd only ever witnessed once before that drug deal with Uncle Cliff stares back. She's still not my favorite person in the world, but Mikey's calm reassurance assails me as I consider my dead parents.

"She's our mother," he'd say, much against my adamant refusal of even mentioning her. *"Forgive her."*

I had no idea where my twin brother was anymore, and while his absence clears my mind, it widens the void in my heart to think of never being able to connect with him again.

He, like my withholding father and abusive mother, is gone.

"Don't cry baby." Devin coos while wrapping his arms around me. "I know these are happy tears, but I hate the sight of you crying or in any kind of pain. It makes me crazy."

I shake my head at the utter misunderstanding. These were far from happy tears. "Dev, I don't think I can do this."

He rubs my back. "You can do this. You got this. We're Carlson's, remember? Carlson's are strong. They don't quit when they're too scared."

I wrap arms around him before blubbering, "But we're not really Carlson's. At least, I'm not. When I look into that mirror all I see is the parents who'd wanted nothing to do with me. Who thought of me as little more than something to sell."

He squeezed me tight. "Stop it, Von. Don't you see it? You're the strongest of any of us. You're the person who ties everyone together. What would this farm look like without you? Or Mamma Dean? Even me..."

"I'm nothing, Devin. Nothing at all. I feel like this imposter with Kimmy. Like if she looks too deep inside, she'll see who I really am. The darkness and destruction that follows me and wrecks every sense of normal and peace. I won't drag her through that."

"Listen to me, and you listen to me real good. Okay?" He says, his tone hard with emotion. "You are everything to me. My sanity. Like you always been. How can you say you're nothing? I did...uh, a lot of reflecting this morning. And I'll tell you something a good friend told me about healing."

"Yeah?" I ask, eager for his wisdom I'd always cherished throughout the years but also apprehensive.

He took a deep breath before pulling us apart. "We've got to get out of this habit of blaming ourselves for the torture our parents put us through. That house we grew up in, in DC, was just a house, and you know it. This here—" He indicates the room with his arms, "is our home. And you have every damn right to have a place in it. Because without you, there's no magic. I see the way Kimmy looks at you and I'm sure she sees the same thing I see."

I stare quizzically at him, my tongue choking me from asking the question.

Devin recenters on me with a huge Cooper grin. "Someone meaningful. You the truth, baby girl, and don't you fucking forget it. Okay?"

I can't fight the smile on my face as I hug him with all my might. This was what I needed to ease some of this pain. To erase the shame of my existence I'd always carried. But the consternation is still mixed in with my doubts as I consider Kimmy's words from last night.

"There's something you should know." She uttered nervously in bed against my raging heart.

"What is it?" I asked, afraid and curious.

She gulped before ruining any sense of trust and peace I felt in that moment with her.

"Mikey told me about a memory from when you guys were little. Said your dad would take him on work trips and errands in New York and New Jersey. He mentioned a tall kid introducing himself as his brother when he went with Quincy on an errand. He didn't recall specifics but remembered sitting inside an all-black car and a child sneaking inside after Quincy left to run his errand. The little boy introduced himself as Shamel and said he was his brother. Your brother."

The world blurred momentarily as I listened to her confession. This couldn't be...

"Are you telling me what I think you're telling me? That you knew about Zay the whole time?"

She shook her head, panicked. "No, no, no. Mikey shared that with me our first time at the lake. But he suspected Zay to be the same boy from that car. I went to Shay yesterday to confront her about it. And...she said it was the truth. That they were really your brother and sister from Camden. She wouldn't give me too many details about it since Zay would 'kill her if he knew she'd told me.' I was going to tell you as soon as I confirmed it babe, I promise."

I didn't argue with her after that. Nope. Just stood up from the bed, ignoring her pleas and questions about where I was going or what I was doing as I left the room to find the front porch. I sat there the entire night, unmoving until the sun rose from the east and guests began to arrive. She didn't follow me and when I returned to the room this morning, she was gone. According to Devin, she and Trice were in one of the guest rooms and doing makeup work.

And here I was, my throat dry as I considered myself in the mirror and arm looped into Devin's.

"Ready to get married, Vonnie Carlson?"

Was I? I asked amidst the doubt swirling inside my chest but gave a tight nod.

The wedding march music could be heard from the yard and my heart skipped as I considered the large crowd of Carlson's awaiting us outside.

The walk to the yard was a rather numb march, but I gulped at the sight when I got to the aisle.

There are so many people I fidget, contemplating dashing out of there. But Devin squeezes my arm.

"I know it's a lot of people. But you got this." He encourages me, and I attempt to slow my breathing as I glance over the crowd we're walking into.

"Right." I agree feebly. And his worried gaze searches the people before I ask, "what's wrong?"

He grunts. "It's Shay. I haven't heard from her since yesterday. And I don't see her here."

I open my mouth to join his bewilderment but shut it when I realize why. I banned Zay from the wedding, and Shay probably took the banishment to apply to her, too. And maybe it does, but her absence still sort of stings as I search the crowd again.

Amongst the sea of brown faces, the sight of a lethal looking image catches my eye.

An Asian man is sitting in the back row, and beside him an equally strange woman with shoulder length dreadlocks. They're the only two I don't recognize and who aren't sharing the same silly smiles of the wedding party. A latent sense of danger lingers in my chest before I hear a baby's cry.

My eyes flick over to the woman I berated last night.

Trice is wearing a yellow getup that makes her look gorgeous, but the fussy baby in her arms makes her stand up, mumble a quick "sorry," before running inside the house.

Devin places a tender kiss on my forehead when we reach the preacher from Mamma Dean's home church.

"Good luck, sis." He whispers before taking a seat in the front row beside Mamma Dean.

Another few minutes tick by, and I'm still nervous and doubtful by the time the crowd stands up.

Kimmy is the most captivating image of perfection under all the Virginia sun as she makes her way down the aisle. Her red curls are tied back in a messy but elegant braid and her white form-fitting dress makes her look like something from a catalog.

She's absolutely stunning. Gorgeous. So many words rush to the surface of my brain, but the only one I can verbalize when she finally stands before me is straight from my heart.

"Kimberly," I breathe, entranced by the red-headed woman with scorching green eyes.

"Yvonne." She repeats back, her voice meek but tender. "Hi."

A smile curves my face as I take her hand. "Hi."

Pastor Jennings begins his speech and I'm barely registering his words as the world fades away from view, leaving only Kimmy in its stead.

"I do." Kimmy whispers after some time, smiling at me.

A moment passes before she asks, "Vonnie?"

"I..." I mutter, hesitating and hating myself for it right now. Here. Of all places. "I...um..."

A rustle from one of the tall bushes behind the archway steals my attention. A person, a guy, bursts forth through the thicket of green and collapses clumsily onto the ground.

"I object!" He slurs, and I'm just now noticing the liquor bottle in his hand.

Kimmy turns and screams. "Jeremy! Is that you?"

"Son!" Vivian calls, rising and running over to the blabbering guy on the ground. "What the hell is going on? You said you didn't want to attend your sister's wedding."

He slaps her assisting hand away while hobbling to his feet. "Course I wanna be here! She's my sister. And I love her."

"Ugh," Kimmy groaned, her face twisted as she approached him. "Are you drunk?"

"Nah!" He said, giggling and taking another long swig from the bottle. The crowd is stirring by now. "Just a little thirsty. Took it from dear old Mamma Dean's stash."

Gasps and shocked stares, including my own, pin on Mamma Dean.

A guilty grimace twists her face, and she stares at me. "That's not, I mean it is—but I was only keeping it for a rainy day. I was never gonna drank it."

"Mamma..." I breathed in horror.

My mouth is hanging wide open at my sweet granny who'd pledged a twenty-year oath to sobriety.

Devin stans, glaring at him. "Get out of here, man. I won't hesitate to beat your ass for ruining my sister's day."

Jeremy threw his head back while cackling. "I come in peace, big brother. Or shall I say, brother number two?"

"What you talkin' bout?" Devin drawls, glancing between me and Jeremy. "Are you crazy or something?"

"Only a little," he chuckled, sipped, and added, "I'm talking about her other brother."

"How do you know Mikey?" He demanded coldly. Devin was losing it, I could feel it, but before I can interject another voice joins the reality TV drama that was becoming my wedding.

"It's me, DC." Zay's voice cuts in as he and a beautifully dressed Shay approach from around the house. "I'm Vonnie's brother."

"And I'm your sister." Shay addressed only me, and I can hear her intermittent sobs from where I'm standing. "I'm sorry, Yvonne. We should have told you so much sooner."

Devin rears back, rubbing his head from the bewilderment of their confessions. "What the fuck is going on around here? Shay, Zay, you're saying that my sister Yvonne is...*your* sister, too?"

"Yes." Zay, who's wearing a sleek black suit and tie, answers. "Shay and I are Quincy's kids from his first marriage. The family he never told y'all about."

Devin's legs staggered as he collapsed into the chair. "I don't believe what I'm hearing right now. How? Just how is this possible?"

Shay speaks up. "Dev, baby, I know this is...weird to hear. This is why I can't accept your proposal. There's just too much old demons that won't let me say yes."

"Proposal?" Trice asks, her eyes swollen and puffy as she returns to the standing crowd of people confronting each other. "What's going on?"

Shay glares at my brother's ex, who's holding Rome. "Who the hell are you?"

Trice frowns at her as she spits back, "And just who the fuck are you? And why is she talking about a proposal?" The last question was meant for my big brother, whose face has turned a pale color as he witnesses the standoff.

"Bad word, Mommy!" A little girl admonishes Trice from the sea of chattering people, and my mind is swirling at the noise that's getting louder and louder until a sharp *bang* rings out in the air.

A gunshot.

From Jeremy, nonetheless, and he growls at the scrambling crowd, "Nobody better fucking move or I'll shoot."

"Jeremy!" Kimmy pleads. "Why? Why are you doing this?"

Jeremy throws the bottle into a bush before aiming the gun at the crowd.

"Him." He sneers, and I realize it's not the crowd he's poising the gun at, but a man.

It's Cousin Dan.

"Hold on there, son." Cousin Dan drawls in warning as he raises his hands. "Watch where you're aiming that thing."

"Oh, I am." Jeremy laughs maniacally as he approaches his uncle with predatory focus. "This is why I'm here. I decided I wouldn't let a rapist dictate whether or not I show up to my only sister's wedding."

Gasps ring out before Kimmy hollers, "What are you talking about? Uncle Dan isn't a rapist. Jeremy, you're drunk. Go in the house and get cleaned up."

Kimmy reached for his arm, but he shrugs her away and turns the gun on her.

"No!" I lurch forward.

"Back up!" He growls as I wrap my entire body around Kimmy, standing in the line of fire should he decide to shoot.

"Come on," I say to her, who begrudgingly lets me drag her away from the deranged animal she called brother.

"Jeremy!" Zay barked. "Don't do this man. I told you to let this shit go. You can't take this man's life; it'll fuck you up for real. I know you think it's a good idea right now, but if you do this you can't ever take it back. Think about it, bro."

Jeremy shakes his head as if to clear it of any remaining humanity before repositioning the gun at Cousin Dan's face. "Tell them, Ma."

Viv looks at her son nervously but doesn't obey.

"Fucking tell them what this man did to you! Tell them why you ran away from home after having me. Tell your precious Mamma Dean your mother's brother was raping you since you turned thirteen. Ain't that right?"

"Son," Viv whimpers, her hands splayed out and sobs shaking her body. "Don't do this, please. He's garbage, I know, but please don't ruin your life like this…"

"Granma Stevie told me when we moved down here." He began, the gun just about shoved into Cousin Dan's mewling mouth. "And it's no wonder why you wanted to bulldoze that house when we got here. How were you supposed to live with the reminder of what he did to you within those walls? Granny told me she knew about Uncle Dan raping you. Said you told her about it right after having me, but she chose to believe this piece of *shit* instead of her own daughter! So, Zay, that thing about killing and not being able to take it back? I've already checked that box."

An eerie horror settles over me before I ask, "Jeremy, please tell me you didn't? I refuse to believe you did something that awful."

Jeremy sneered. "Refuse to believe I didn't smother that old bitch with her pillow after she told me about it? That's your prerogative then. She's no granny of mine if she believed this trash over her own daughter."

"Lord, help me!" Mamma Dean uttered, clutching her chest. "Not my Stevie. Not my Stevie..."

"Jeremy...why?" Kimmy demanded. "You're drunk. That's it. You wouldn't have done that to Granma Stevie. You're just trying to scare us."

"Believe what you want, but I'm sick of pretending. I left Gavin's house yesterday and made the drive to do this. I couldn't leave this alone. I'm here to do what Shame refused to do, even after I hired him to do it."

"Shame?" Kimmy queried. "Who's Shame?"

"Me." Zay responded sullenly. "That's the name I went by when I lived in Camden. Jeremy and I know each other from Jersey."

"That's right." Jeremy cosigned. "He was the guy you went to for contracts like this. But, apparently, he had a change of heart since reuniting with his *baby sis*." He puts a mocking emphasis on 'baby sis,' that makes me want to punch him.

Memories assail me just then, and I recall Jeremy's phone call with Zay in the bathroom, of how strange it was that he laughed at me for calling him the "fucking shame." Quincy's babblings when he possessed Kimmy also bring on a new clarity, too: *Shame...all because of Shame. Shame, shame, shame!*

There was so much wrong done in the dark, and I'm overcome with the desire to just run away. But I don't. I stand there with Kimmy in my arms, trying to be her peace instead of her turmoil in all this.

Jeremy cocks the gun inside Cousin Dan's mouth. "He's our father, Kim."

"No!" Kimmy hollers. "Stop lying. You're drunk!"

"Kimmy." Viv's voice warbles from her seat. She's still crying as she nods, confirming Jeremy's accusation.

"What...Uncle Dan is...?" Kimmy stutters, clutching me tight.

"Our father, that's right." Jeremy finishes. "Any last words, old man? Before I blow your fucking brains out?"

Things move in somewhat of a slow motion as the tensions rises.

Zay, yells, "No! Jeremy, man don't do this shit!"

Kimmy wrestles me within the confines of my arms, but I don't budge. She swats me angrily as she snarls, "Get off me! I have to stop him from ruining his life."

"He's done enough of that already, babe. Please, just stop. Be still."

"No!" She shrieks.

Mamma Dean is wailing and begging the Lord to forgive her, Devin is glancing between Shay, Trice, and me, as if he's not sure if he can protect us all at the same time. Kale, my brother's former friend and Trice's husband, enfolds a child in his arms as he huddles away from the scene.

And then it happens. The thing we all fear actually comes to pass as the single round of gunfire pierces the air again.

"No!" Viv screams, but not because her only son shot her rapist uncle.

"RICHMOND POLICE!" The boys in blue rush through the yard ceremony, stomping on carefully placed flowers and decor as they aim guns at the crowd. "Everybody freeze with your hands in the air. Not one movement!"

"My baby!" Viv groans from the ground over Jeremy's lurching body. She strokes his hair. "Y'all shot my son!"

Cousin Dan, relieved, scurries onto the ground and raises his hands in the air, abiding to the police's demands.

Kimmy and I are standing with our hands raised as we studied her brother's body jerk violently. Blood is pouring from his mouth and he's staring absently at us. There's a single gunshot hole in his white shirt where the blood is leaking from.

"K-Kim?" He sputters weakly.

"Jeremy..." she sobs. "Don't move too much!! You'll make the bleeding worse."

He coughs up blood as he laughs. "I won't make it outta this alive. Ain't that a son of a bitch..."

The cops are rounding everyone up and escorting them to the front yard. Everyone but a few people hang back, including Zay, Shay, Devin, and the two lethal looking strangers I observed from earlier.

The Asian man stands up, calm and collected as if there aren't law officials barking commands at the rest of the crowd in the front yard.

"Nice seeing you again, Shame." The Asian guy addresses Zay, whose face has turned a ghostly color.

Shay looks equally horrified, but also a little confused as she stares at the black, petite woman with him.

"Jerica?" She questions in a panicked hiss. "How are you here right now?"

Jerica looks to the Asian man, as if for permission to speak. He offers one tight nod.

"Y'all gotta come back to Jersey. Please."

"You both should heed her advice, Shame and Shayne. It's time to pay back the money you owe."

Asian dude states, so cold and matter-of-fact, that I'm compelled to watch it play out.

However, something so unexpected happens that makes me question the kinds of demons awaiting them in Jersey.

Shay and Zay shared a long, exploratory look before bolting through the trees together. Effectively leaving me with the dying brother of my almost-wife and family.

The police are still rounding people up and a lone officer dips low to yank Viv away from Jeremy's now still body.

"No!" She hollers, a shrill sound only mother's who'd lost their children could make. "Please don't take my baby away from me!"

Kimmy darts over to help her mom, but the officer holds her back.

I move to defuse the situation, to make sense of all this *Lifetime Movie Network* drama that won't cease to end, when something stops me, dead in my tracks.

No, not something, someone. A presence, and a voice.

"Vonnie!" Mikey calls from inside my mind. *"I'm back."*

AUTHOR'S NOTE

Laura, here! Thank you so much for reading this rather tragic story. Fun fact: Yvonne's story almost never happened, as I felt the bit of mystery of her life was meaningful to the plotline in the REAL series. However, after her character materialized and her feelings for a certain redhead became clear, I felt it an injustice not to give Yvonne's voice a platform. As a token of my appreciation, please enjoy this prelude to *SHAME*, the eighth book in the series.

Love always,
Laura
xoxo

SHAME

"It really is a pity that you're dropping out of school, young man. Is there nothing else we can do to set you up for success?" Counselor Riviera asked cautiously between small bites of her fish bagel.

Well, it looked and smelled like fish, my nose auto-detecting the pink flesh poking out from the sides of it as something belonging to the sea. Fucking nasty is what it was, no doubt about it.

I shifted in the seat opposite of the fat Spanish lady, being careful to hold in my breath a few precious seconds before responding.

"Uh, yeah," I sighed. "The best way to move forward is letting me drop out. Peacefully. And without my parents too deep in the process."

"Peacefully? Any trouble at home? I'd be glad to follow up with your parents if—"

"Not necessary."

Flustered, she took another bite from her smelly fish bagel before lamenting, "Shamel, son, please understand this is a serious matter here. You've exuded nothing less than academic excellence since you began at Marlton High, and it's just my job to counsel you about this possibility."

I tried really fucking hard to keep the barf from coming up, and hardened my face as I stared at her crumby one. "Like I said, Counselor Riviera, that's not necessary. There ain't no problems at home. In fact, my Old Man been nagging me to drop this school shit for a minute now."

"Surely, that isn't true?"

"Too bad it is. And I been fighting it, but now I think it's time I go. Just show me the paperwork necessary to start the process."

"Shamel," she extended her hand to me, her eyes sympathetic. "Can you not hear the problem in that statement?"

"What's the problem?"

"More like, *who's* the problem? Surely, your father is not encouraging you to withdraw from high school. That's unethical."

"Well, I ain't exactly his pride and joy." I respond, my tone flat and withholding. I was more like his shame and fury. And it was true, I thought, as I considered his permanent frown and shitty disposition when it came to me. "But if it's his approval you need, gimme a sec."

"Okay." She agrees as I slide the newest edition iPhone from my denim jean pocket. I dial one of the three numbers saved in the contacts and place the trilling phone on loudspeaker as we wait for it to connect.

"Fuck you want, man?" My old man demands in his usual setting of pissed off.

"Trying to drop out of school. Counselor's giving me a hard time, saying I need your permission, or some shit. You on loudspeaker and I'm in her office."

I anticipate the fury behind his next retort. "Tell that bitch I said you want out. Yesterday. And to send me any paperwork needed to make that happen. Understand?"

"Yep." I met her eyes, which were round with shock.

"I'm talking to your teacher, not you boy. Do you understand what I'm saying?"

"Y-Yes, Mr. Masters," she stammered in embarrassment while wiping the crumbs off her face. "Loud and clear."

"Good." he sneers. "Now don't call me again unless it's an emergency." He hangs up without a goodbye, Commander style, and an action I've long since stopped getting in my feelings about.

"So." I begin. "We good here?"

"Shamel, I really wish—"

"I'm trying to play this shit nice!" I stood up, pissed at her protests but also unable to be in the presence of that nasty fish sandwich she devoured minutes ago. "Gimme the papers, or I'll get them myself. I ain't come to you for counseling. Or your pity talk. Or your disappointment. Fuck all that."

"Excuse me?!"

"Nah, excuse *me*. I gotta find somebody who actually can do their job without all the fucking condescending ass, gentle ass, third degree."

She's sputtering and hurling threats my way as I turn to the door.

Somehow, her enraged scolding puts me in mind of my old man whenever I returned home with the unsold product he placed in my charge to move, and a dark smile curves my lips as I exit the office. Waste of talent, she calls it? A pity? Nah, I operated with ease in the shadows and took pride in people's general lack of faith in me. Maybe my ties to the real monsters on these gritty Camden streets was my downfall, but if I went down, at least the fall wouldn't be alone or in vain. I had a mission, and I dedicated my next few years to seeing that shit through for a change.

Was it a pity to be dropping out of this under-funded dank ass school? Maybe.

Was it a waste to be leaving the only home and family I ever knew to start this mission? Possibly.

Was it worth it? Hell fucking yeah.

Pity played a huge part in me dropping the "L" in my government name so that I could live and profit comfortably from the shadows.

Ain't that a shame? Yeah, that's me, and you'd best learn not to forget it.

ABOUT THE AUTHOR

Since the age of twelve, Laura could always be found writing. She writes within a wide array of genres, including paranormal, drama, slice of life, and (her favorite) romance. In her free time, if she's not writing, she's reading or listening to a steamy audio-book. Her most notable works include Something About Kyle and her ongoing, The REAL Series, which explores the narratives of various, interconnected young adults.

As an author, Laura aims to push boundaries and leave a lasting impact on her community. Her journey taught her the importance of persever-ance, creativity, and staying true to one's unique vision. Support her craft by purchasing from her bookstore.